Sha
Shames, Germaine W.
Between two deserts : a
    novel $ 24.00

BETWEEN TWO DESERTS

A Novel by
Germaine W. Shames

MacAdam/Cage Publishing
155 Sansome Street, Suite 550
San Francisco, CA 94104
www.macadamcage.com

Library of Congress Cataloging-in-Publication Data

Shames, Germaine W.
    Between two deserts / by Germaine W. Shames.
        p. cm.
    ISBN 1-931561-13-3 (alk. paper)
    1. Americans–Jerusalem–Fiction. 2. Young women–Fiction.
    3. Jerusalem–Fiction. I. Title.

PS3619.H354 B47 2002
813'.6–dc21

                                                        200205970

Manufactured in the United States of America.
10 9 8 7 6 5 4 3 2 1

Book and jacket design by Dorothy Carico Smith.

BETWEEN TWO DESERTS

A Novel by
Germaine W. Shames

MacAdam/Cage

*To the memory of my parents,
and for those who loved them best.*

For La.

I believe in the doctrine of nonviolence as a weapon
of the weak. I believe in the doctrine of nonviolence
as a weapon of the strongest. I believe that a man
is the strongest soldier for daring to die unarmed.

Mohandes Gandhi

Hold always the sign of blood in horror.
Take care not to shed or stain thyself with it,
for the mark is never washed away.

Salah-ah-Din; advice to his son, Dhahir

Enough of blood and tears. Enough.

Yitzhak Rabin

MAP OF THE HUMAN HEART

W hen, boarding his first airplane, Abie Baron died of a massive coronary, his granddaughter, Eve Cavell, inherited 1,237 maps, 360 back issues of *National Geographic*, and an unused Pan Am ticket to Lod, Israel. Eve would not have expected her grandfather, a fervent atheist, to begin his wanderings in the land of Zion. But then, when had Abie ever conformed to her—or anyone else's—expectations?

"You put your dreams on hold all those years thinking there's a white line painted down the middle of every road," he had lamented, holding on to life just long enough to watch the 747 taxi down the runway without him. "Sometimes there's no road at all."

Once Eve had a heart like a pinwheel spinning free of its axis. This was how she'd picture it, when as a girl her grandfather would lift her in his mighty arms and whirl her in a circle without beginning or end. Her imagination unbound. Abie, as big as the world.

Shayna maydala, he would call her, beautiful little girl, while her head spun and all the wonder of life coursed through her.

Each time Abie acquired a new map, he would spread it open on the living room carpet and crawl around its periphery on all fours, reading aloud the place-names that piqued his fancy.

"Maputo...Devil's Island...Uxmal...the Sea of Cortez...Isn't that where Steinbeck bagged all the marine life? Did he ever stop to think that gilled creatures might have a soul? No, he just hauled it all in like flotsam." Abie's brow furrowed. His hand swept across the Atlantic Ocean. "Cameroon...Broken Hill...Cape Karikari..."

Eve never tired of hearing the names.

"Now you, *shayna maydala*," he said, "you pick."

Lisping through the gap where her front teeth should have been, she answered, "Jerusalem."

It was the longest word she knew at the time, and the most mysterious. A man in a flowing black coat and bologna curls had confided it to her while waiting turns in a Kosher butcher shop.

"Jerusalem," Abie echoed. Then, quoting Amichai, "All these stones, all this sadness, all this light."

Eve, still dressed in mourning, touches down on the hallowed tarmac of Ben-Gurion Airport with Abie's chimeric presence hovering about her like a summer fog. No map has prepared her for the headiness of soaring off the edge of a continent. She feels unclasped. She misses her grandfather's weight and bulk, the surefooted, bearish man he had been only days before. Time hurtles her forward faster than she can calculate her losses.

Her destination decided, she doesn't linger in Lod. Dimly conscious of having become a foreigner, a sensation not unlike dreaming, she boards a collective taxi, closes her eyes, and opens them to the glare of morning.

Lost for the light, she takes a first squint-lidded measure of Jerusalem. To the west a trio of boy soldiers doze over rifles. To the east the dispossessed crouch in doorways, rattling worry beads. History's unsparing passage etched into the stones, into faces, and every street a fragile seam relentlessly fraying.

She records her impressions in a black leather-bound journal. It comforts her, when the sirens wail, to flip back through the pages and remind herself that one day follows the next. To begin a fresh entry bolsters her resolve.

Having abandoned her position as Foreign Student Advisor of a New England college and taken her dreams out of cold storage, she has decided to become what she was always meant to be: a poet.

The fact that she has never actually written a poem, that she lacks even the rudiments of craft, doesn't deter her. The verses, she is convinced, have been gestating in her soul ever since Abie first showed her a photograph of the sun setting over the Dome of the Rock. Eve caches her fevered scribblings between the covers of her journal, but each time she leaves the pages unattended her grandfather—now her sole critic as well as her sole companion—will strike an adjective or correct her spelling. She recognizes his handwriting, defiantly large, lifting off the lines in whimsical loops and tails.

Shunning the luxury hotels, she sublets a flat on the edge of the Muslim Quarter, its only asset a view nearly identical to the one she has held in her mind's eye since childhood. The rooms are of stone, and so old that the walls lean. The passageways house a multitude of ghosts. Over time she grows fond of them, rising in the blue-edged darkness of predawn to record their voices. She writes by candlelight. As the sun rises, her grandfather blows out the flame.

"Hurry, *shayna maydala,*" he chides her, "we didn't come all the way to Jerusalem to hole up in a garret with a bunch of deadbeats."

Eve closes her journal and places it in a tote bag along with a yellowed map of the Old City and a slim volume of Kabir's two-line verse. Moving in synchrony, ghost and granddaughter descend the staircase and emerge into the flurry of morning. The day's first headlines—hollow odes to child martyrs and historical mandates—begin to buzz through the streets like swarming bees. Merchants crank open the shutters of their shops. Already crowds are streaming toward the souk.

Since the rioting broke out in Gaza and the West Bank, there's no telling when the bazaar's myriad shops will be open. A faceless entity calling itself The Unified Committee of the Uprising has begun to disperse leaflets throughout East Jerusalem calling for general strikes, boycotts, blood. Only yesterday the soldiers came for her

3

neighbor's son.

"Step lively," Abie says, pressing ahead despite the arthritis in his knees.

Shoppers and pilgrims, all with the same laminated eyes, hasten by her as she makes her way up the timeworn steps of David Street. Donkey dung lies in sorry little heaps among the cobblestones. Five thousand years of warring idols and unheard prayers hum beneath her feet. Hawkers call out to her, their tongues thick with flattery, but she has lost touch with the living; the dead, at least, don't lie.

She passes through the cavernous arch of Jaffa Gate, pausing a moment to cool her cheek against the stone. In the distance she hears the hoarse voice of a street preacher, "The Lord your God is coming with a strong arm!" Always the same bullying scripture. She steps out into the sunlight and sees the preacher mop his forehead with a tattered handkerchief, flies adhering to the loose threads of his linen tunic like bits of lint.

"Wretched fellow's come unglued," she hears Abie whisper.

Setting down her tote bag on a low stone wall, she sits, draws out her journal, and turns her head up. Her eyes close. She begins to write, *Poor messenger one-groove, the desert rats have eaten away your sacred robes*...Conjuring grace in a wilderness of words, she mends what time has torn, the street preacher no longer a crazy man in a burlap sack but a wounded prophet. With a stroke of her pen she reknits the warp and woof of his spirit. He stands upright, and swears he can see salvation run through the streets like a naked child.

In the distance a *muezzin* calls the righteous to prayer with his ululating chant. Eve closes the journal and opens her eyes. Motionless in her shadow stands a young man, tall, with arching eyebrows and vaulted cheekbones, staring into her face as if to unmask it.

"You're a *houri*," he says, continuing to stare without apology.

Eve takes cover behind a pair of horn-rimmed sunglasses that once belonged to her grandfather. She studies the intruder, riveted by the fire in his green eyes, whole forests of cypress and pine ablaze between the thick fringes of lash.

Unabashed, the young man repeats, "A *houri*, the beautiful woman who waits in paradise."

That evening as Eve prepares for bed, soaking in the clawfooted bathtub that has become her refuge, Abie comes to her in a cloud of steam, saying, "I'm leaving now."

The bathwater, hot only a moment before, makes her pores gape. Trailing soap bubbles, she follows her grandfather into the corridor.

"Coming?" he calls over his shoulder, his dear wrinkled face a glimmer in the gathering penumbra.

"But...but we haven't been to Rachel's Tomb or climbed the Mount of Olives." She reaches out for him with fingers pulsing. "Why don't you come back inside, it's so cold out here."

Water drips down her limbs, forming icy puddles at her feet.

"Old tombs, old walls...Where's the present hiding?"

"But our roots are here—isn't that why we came?"

"Roots?" he sighs.

Eve sighs in turn. Daughter of a blended marriage, mother Jewish, father a lapsed Catholic, her origins have also had more breadth than depth.

"I came to see what all the brouhaha was about. Truth is, I never quite trusted Cecil B. De Mille. How do you cast a Moses, or part the Red Sea without making it look like a remake of *Moby Dick*?"

"Stay."

"Life is for the living, *shayna maydala*," Abie says, his once resonant voice little more than an echo. "I waited too long. Don't you make the same mistake. That young suitor of yours—he's smitten, you know. I only wish I could leave you a map of the human heart."

A sudden wind thrusts shut the door. Eve's naked body arcs forward, frozen, glistening in the flicker of a single bare bulb.

"Oh, grandpa," she whispers, "I'll never be ready to lose you."

Leaving on her pillow the landslides of memory, Eve rises and throws back the gauze curtain. Stray dogs prowl the gutter for splinters of bone. A wayward wind blows chewing gum wrappers and sunflower seed husks down the crooked lane.

As she watches, an old man—European, judging by the cut of his pants and his waxed handlebar mustache—peers up at her window. There's something vaguely familiar about him, though Eve can't place him. The forward tilt of his posture, his paunch perhaps, reminds her of Abie. He stands on the street corner shuffling his feet. He looks up once again. For a moment their gazes lock, then he lowers his bearish head and walks hurriedly away.

"One more ghost," she thinks.

She crosses the room to the wardrobe, opens it, and begins to take down the black dress that has become her uniform since her grandfather's death. On an impulse, she shunts the garment into a corner and dresses instead in the colors of ripening—gold, sienna, carmine. She paints her lips. Her reflection in the mirror smiles, a tentative smile, then the tears jar loose and trickle unchecked into the corners of her mouth.

With the taste of salt on her tongue, she descends the staircase and steers a course toward Jaffa Gate. Her grandfather's absence hangs in the air like smoke from a doused fire. She makes her way up David Street, pausing every so often to admire a piece of embroidery, a rare flower, a persimmon...touching these things. Many of the Arab merchants seem to know her. They greet her by name with a decorous flourish of the arm, but their offers of tea and treasures can't detain her. The memory of the young man's eyes draws her on. She can't resist their lure any more than a sieve can keep out the desert.

Wisps of cloud skim along the ramparts. The gate comes into view, casting into shadow the tourists, hawkers, and Hassids who mill about its flanks. Amid the din of car horns and jackhammers, she hears the preacher cry, "The Lord your God is coming…"

Distracted, for a moment she fails to notice the small well-groomed boy—not more than six or seven years old—who has grafted himself onto her skirts. Dressed in a school uniform though the schools have been closed for weeks, he tugs for attention at the hem of her blouse.

"S'cuse me, lady."

Eve stops and gazes down at him. She smiles. But gradually, as the boy's features come into focus, her lips lose their arc. She takes an unsteady step backward.

"Me freedom fighter," he boasts loudly. Then repeats, for the benefit of his peers, "*Ana fedaye.*"

Grabbing her hand, he pops his right eye—glass—into the palm, as if it were a fallen baby tooth.

She tries to speak but can only emit monosyllables: "No—God—why?"

With an upward toss of his chin, he snatches the prosthesis from her and holds it aloft so that the stationary pupil seems to stare directly into her eyes. She half turns but her gaze, growing softer and sadder with every heartbeat, remains fixed on the boy's mutilated face. The tote bag holding her cache of poems drops to the ground. As she kneels to retrieve it, a second boy, older, steals up beside her, so close he might whisper in her ear.

"*Ana fedaye!*" he cries.

She feels the souk dim around her, the colors fade to gray. The baubles and talismans, the heaped spices, the pyramids of Jaffa oranges…lose definition, lie forlorn like underexposed black-and-white photographs. She is aware of absence. An absence the size of her grandfather, as big as the world.

"*Imshi*," she hears a male voice say sternly, "go away."

"You go way, *Inglise.*" The defaced boy raises his empty eye socket in a final gesture of defiance before taking his friend by the arm and disappearing into the crowd.

Eve looks up to find the portly old European hovering over her, his face ruddy above the waxed mustache, pale beneath it, one hairy hand extended toward her in a gesture of succor.

"Come," he says in a deep, gentle voice hinting at an accent she's heard before but can't identify.

Her vision blurs with tears. She feels him take her by the arm and lead her back toward the Muslim Quarter.

"Cry, *shayna maydala*," he says, as if speaking to a child.

He extracts an oversized cotton handkerchief from his back pocket and presses it into her hand.

For a time they walk in silence, the old man meandering, holding tight to her sleeve. Where he will take her, she has no clue. By this time most of the shops are shuttered. Here and there a door stands ajar, attended from a distance by a nervous merchant violating the early closing hours dictated by the Unified Committee. Passersby too look uneasy. Somewhere between the Via Dolorosa and Lion's Gate, he stops and, absently purling the tips of his mustache, pivots a full 360 degrees.

"There's a place I go," she volunteers, beginning now to lead him.

He follows willingly, huffing softly from exertion.

"These old stones…" he murmurs.

"They speak."

"It's not the stones speaking," he corrects her in a whisper, "but the dead. Where there's no forgiveness, no one finds rest."

At a branch of the road she hesitates, gazing in one direction then the other before taking the less trodden of the ways. The old man pauses to catch his breath. They pass beneath an archway and enter a grassy courtyard. To one side a sunken pool casts back a murky reflection of the clouds. Gesturing toward it, she says, "People come here to be healed."

They stand at the edge of the pool, the old man fidgeting with his mustache, Eve watching him with curiosity. Stiff-jointed, he inclines forward, stopping just short of a bow.

"Mozes Koenig, at your disposition."

"Eve Cavell."

"Eve," he echoes, gazing down at her image. "But, how much like my Gizella you look…"

She nudges him lightly on the shoulder and steers him to a weather-beaten bench shaded by orange trees. A vague smile plumps out his cheeks. Using the cuff of his sleeve, he wipes the bench's wooden slats, then gestures for her to sit.

"Tell me," she says, "tell me about Gizella."

His smile fades, replaced by an expression whose meaning she can only guess at. Wrinkles score his brow like minus signs, like roads ending.

"There was a time, *shayna maydala*, when the world was all of one piece. Fresh bread on the table, goosedown pillows on the bed. The mornings smelled of elderflowers blooming…the scent of Gizella's hair. She wore it in a braid during the day, but at night she would let it down, whole handfuls of it spilling across the sheets. Dark, like yours."

"Who was she?"

"My wife, of course," he says. "She was seventeen when we married, but already wise. She knew how to cast spells with candles and blades of grass. My family thought her strange, uncultured. They didn't understand how a woman could read a book without opening its cover."

"Second sight?"

He goes on, as if he's not heard her.

"Gizella saw it all coming...the pogroms, the rise of Hitler, the splintering of our lives. In the middle of winter—I'll never forget that morning, fog so thick I thought I'd never come out the other side of it—she had me bundle our twin sons in a horsehair blanket and take them outside the city to live with the gentiles. She knew the Nazis were on their way and that the boys wouldn't survive otherwise. She tried to warn my parents, her own, the neighbors. No one would listen to her. *Mishugenah*, they called her, crazy. Poor Mozes, married to such a woman. But I believed her. When she told me to leave my sons with the peasant family, I obeyed without question; when she told me to go off with the Partisans, I did that too. And today, my sons are alive, and I've muddled through to tell the story."

"And Gizella?"

"Oh, how Gizella dreamed of Jerusalem! She described it all to me—the light, the honeysuckle, the way the wind tastes when it races down the Mount of Olives."

"She must be happy here."

"She's dead," he says tonelessly. "She saved everyone but herself."

Eve lays her head on the old man's shoulder, as she used to do with her grandfather, and feels a pang of something at once sweet and agonizing. They belong here, she and this wandering stranger with the biblical name, two souls searching for the seam that joins the past to the present, the dead to the living.

Nearby, a young man on crutches tosses a coin into the pool, rippling its surface. Mozes Koenig rouses himself with a sigh.

"At my age, the mind plays tricks," he says in a tone of apology, paw-like hands gesturing without object. "One sees ghosts everywhere."

She would like to reassure the old man, to tell him that his ghosts are real, that Jerusalem makes ghosts even of the young, but instead she says, "You too remind me of someone."

Eve wends her way to Jaffa Gate, the sun high and a cavalcade of wounded spirits—pilgrims, housewives, storefront messiahs—streaming alongside her. She takes her place on the low wall, a southerly wind lifting the plaits of hair from her shoulders without cooling them. In the distance she sees, or imagines she sees, the young man with the incendiary gaze. Like the desert storm he waits for his moment, already hers.

Opening her journal, she glances at a fresh entry, not a poem but a message, scrawled in the singular loops and flourishes that only her grandfather could have penned.

It's a saying from the Torah sages, and the one truth Abie had forgotten to tell her: "The wholest heart is the one that has been broken."

THE LAST MESSENGER

"The Lord your God is coming with a strong arm!" cries the stooped man in the homespun tunic, voice cracking like clay pigeons left in too hot a kiln. Sweat drips into his eyes. He thinks of Christ on the cross, baking in the Judean sun—this very same sun—for hours, days, no one daring to shade his ravaged face.

Nearby, a dispersed band of hungry-fisted waifs hawk their wares. "Twenty postcard, two shekel!"

Their raised voices trouble the messenger. They are not Christian voices, tempered by hymns and the Lord's Prayer, but the howl of jackals, the bleating of goats…He cups palms to his ears.

"The Lord your God is coming with a strong arm," he calls again, straining to amplify the words, "repent and be saved, for soon it will be too late."

He has become a fixture on this cobbled thoroughfare leading to Jerusalem's Old City. Crowds stream by him without raising an eyebrow. He must resist the urge to tug at their sleeves. Squinting into the sun, he clasps hands behind his back and stands straight and still as a monument to bone.

"Repent and be saved, for soon it will be too late."

A scraggly-haired passerby—American, the messenger deduces based on the battered state of the man's designer jeans—pauses just long enough to retort, "It's already too late."

That the messenger is surrounded by cynics, heathen, adulterers, he accepts as part of God's plan. Satan's servants, cooing over the airwaves, leering down from billboards, promise the masses heaven without redemption. He has seen the lines at the automatic teller machines, at the R-rated movie houses. Prophesy unfolding.

Jerusalem, one more den of sin. And now this barbaric rioting, the Arab youth out of control, the mothers rabid. He feels the end coming, and the urgency of his mission makes his lungs swell.

"The Lord your God is coming with…twenty postcard."

The child merchants seek shade at the mouth of Jaffa Gate. Yawning, their young bodies lank as weeds, they lean against the cool stone.

"Lost souls," the messenger murmurs to himself, flicking the sweat from his forehead with an ink-stained hand.

He has begun to copy passages from the Bible in his own writ. It soothes him, when he can't sleep or a yellow wind makes his head throb. In the margins he scribbles notes about the people he sees at the gate, strangers whose lives he reconstructs like an archaeologist charting lost worlds from rubble.

There is the young Jewish woman with the tragic face, who carries a leather journal and makes entries in it with her eyes closed. The children call her Eve. She has spoken to him, to ask the time or comment about the heat. Her voice stirs something vaguely unwholesome in him. Sometimes he pretends he hasn't heard her and walks away. But at night he catches himself thinking about her, imagining her nakedness and the way she arches her back at the height of rapture. Rendered sleepless by the vileness of his thoughts, he picks up his pen and writes, "In the beginning," and keeps on until Adam has sunk his teeth into the apple and the rising sun spills across the tired scrawl of words.

This Jewish woman—may Jesus chasten her—has fallen into the web of a Muslim Don Juan. The messenger has watched the young Arab prowl the gate, starched pelvis probing. How many dewy-eyed tourists has he carried off? The messenger has lost count. But Eve is not the young man's usual prey. The others have been girls, silly and blonde. Eve has a biblical look about her, Semitic, and her dark eyes hold secrets that could drive a man to perdition. She has to be older than the Arab by five or ten years.

Never far off hovers an ancient bear of a man, a Hungarian, ogling the Jewess like a lovesick schoolboy. Whenever the messenger lets down his guard, the old man summons him with a pudgy index finger and tries to ensnare him in conversation about mysticism or the human condition.

"Why do you repeat the same scripture over and over again?" he demands to know.

To the messenger, the answer could not be more obvious.

"So little time left."

He doesn't tell the Hungarian that God Himself has called him here, that he has abandoned a wife and nine children in Perth, Australia, to deliver this most portentous of messages. Afraid of sounding boastful, unchristian, he doesn't say, I am the Last Messenger.

"But people aren't listening," the Hungarian suggests gently. "They didn't listen to Moses—or Jesus—or Muhammad. You might as well stand on your head reciting Mother Goose."

The old man claps an arm about his shoulder as if to console him. In the distance Eve closes her eyes, and her hands begin to trace arabesques between the covers of her journal.

"That woman," the old man sighs. "Hasn't anyone taught her the price of breaking a taboo?"

The messenger can only shrug his burdened shoulders. He finds it hard to stand upright since he came to Jerusalem, with strangers pinning these cryptic scraps upon him like fetishes, like storm advisories.

At noon sharp he abandons his post and hurries through the Old City to his rented flat in the Armenian Quarter. Routine has always suited him, a time for everything. Lunch at one. Nap at three. He takes a loaf of braided bread from the cupboard and examines it for mold. He takes down a plate. Through the powdery walls he hears his neighbor stifle a sob. Recently widowed, she does not cease to cry day or night and has taken to sleeping with the radio on.

He hears her timid tap at his door.

"For you, yes?" she says in halting English, holding out a plain white envelope with a familiar postmark.

"M'wife's steady as a clock."

Eyes lowered, he takes the letter. The widow forces a smile and retreats with backward steps, a yellow handkerchief clutched to her red eyes.

He places the letter on the kitchen table and prepares lunch: the bread, a dollop of apricot preserves, and a string of Bedouin figs. He eats standing over the kitchen sink, gazing out the window at his neighbor's laundry drying on the clothesline. It occurs to him that he's never seen an item of underwear hanging there, which makes him wonder about the widow and her standards of hygiene. Armenians might be Christians, he reasons, but for centuries they've lived alongside Muslims. Degeneration was inevitable.

Drawing the curtain, he retires to the table and retrieves his wife's letter. She, Ethel, has written to him twice a week since his departure three years ago. The sight of her small tidy script elicits a twinge of fondness. She has enclosed a snapshot of the children, the lot of them arranged in three even rows according to height.

*Matthew made the honor roll. Magda won the prize for perfect attendance again this year. Wish you could see the new crop of parsnips, white as talcum. My brother John helped out with the mortgage payment. The church sent us another boxful of canned goods. The whole congregation prays for your safety...*He skims to the end of the letter, carelessly creasing its edge. *I hide the newspapers from the children. The pictures of the wee Arabs throwing stones at the soldiers were giving them nightmares.* He has read enough.

Replacing the letter in its envelope, he stands, yawns into both hands, and pads into the sleeping nook.

He awakens from his nap feeling cranky, needing to pee. The sun has begun to set behind the Mount of Olives. He has never liked this time of day; its creeping emptiness makes him want to throw open all the windows and gather in the last paltry rays of light. He steps outside to the toilet, hoping the widow won't peek through her slatted window shade, as she always does whenever she hears his footsteps along the corridor. One day he will pass water with the bathroom door wide open, he resolves, serve the busybody right—but not today. As he unzips his fly, he hears her begin to sob once again.

Darkness claims the little flat by minutes, by inches. He paces in front of the windows until the last glimmer has vanished, then turns on the sitting room lamp, removing the shade so that the low-wattage bulb burns brighter. He reaches for his Bible but his eyes refuse to focus on the page. The letters crawl like ants, forming designs suggestive of body parts, unnatural couplings, Eve's quivering bosom in the throes of passion…He squeezes shut his lids.

"I have gone astray, oh Lord, like a lost sheep."

The book slips from his hands. He lumbers to his feet and stands sway-jointed in the middle of the room, aware of gravity pressing in on him, novas exploding above his head.

A moment later he finds himself outside on the street, at a loss to explain how he got there. Stray dogs slink starving through the alleys. Housewives gather on doorsteps to whisper blasphemies in an alien tongue. He doesn't trust the night. Not since Ethel first spoke in her sleep, reciting passages from the Song of Solomon. He slept in the tool shed after that, preferring cold and mice to the nearness of her flesh. Some nights he would wander the streets, as he does now. No destination, only the vague inkling of having stepped beyond grace.

"Like a lost sheep."

The streetlamps grow brighter as he passes the Tower of David and veers north toward the Muslim Quarter. Arab men crouch dull-eyed in doorways, playing backgammon and smoking hookahs. The aromas of chickpea paste and honeysuckle mingle in the humid air like the memory of a forbidden liaison.

Once, even he, the Last Messenger, had known the thrill of plucking a fruit before its time. Lydia had been prematurely endowed, a devilish girl who would raise her skirt for a licorice whip. He hadn't been the first. Years later, once Christ had saved him from a life of dissipation, he swore on his mother's honor to marry a homely girl. His cousin Ethel was flat-chested and a mouth breather. He wed her the way a farmer might add livestock to a pen. He took her home and showed her where he kept the pots and pans and how he liked his eggs cooked, then he turned out the light and deflowered her, holding her still beneath him, promising, "It will be over soon."

The messenger finds himself on an unfamiliar street corner. He stops walking, knowing somehow that he has arrived. In the shadows he makes out the stocky figure of the Hungarian. The old man pretends to wind his wristwatch, but anyone with eyes can see that he's loitering beneath a gauze-curtained window, peeping at the sinful carryings-on of two silhouettes—a man and a woman merging in a flagrant act of fornication.

The street fills with sighs. The messenger watches the couple dance in and out of the light, a dizzying juxtaposition of limbs and lips, fusing, breaking free. He watches the Hungarian crane his neck and mouth curses. A warm breeze blows the curtain aside, revealing the woman's face, dark and feral, her long hair whipping the bed linen like tongues of black flame. Eve, gloriously naked. Eve, as he's dreamed her.

Hunching against the wind, the old Hungarian plods toward

Damascus Gate. His receding back makes the messenger think of barley and saddle leather. The street lies deserted, except for a pair of boy soldiers dozing slit-eyed over automatic rifles. A crescent moon reminds the messenger that the world has never belonged to the righteous.

The light dims in Eve's window. Moments later, the young Arab exits the house sauntering like a racehorse and disappears down a back street.

The messenger prays wordlessly. Jerusalem has worn away the margins of his faith, thrust him within a hair's breadth of despair. He came to her gates on a mission. Day after dreary day he has delivered his message—a hundred times, a thousand—until the syllables lodge in his throat like shards of glass. But still, the chosen build their Sodoms and the others throw their stones. Nobody listens.

Stung by the futility of his calling only to be stung the more fiercely by conviction, he crosses the street, knowing what he must do.

"Oh daughter of Babylon, who art to perish." The words come like a bottle carried on the waves, destined for him alone. "Happy be he who dasheth your little ones against the stones."

The staircase, steep and dark, leads straight to Eve's door. A sliver of light illumines its lower edge—she must still be awake. He bounds up the steps and stands paralyzed on the hemp doormat.

"Salim?" he hears her say.

Her *Arab*, thinks the messenger. The name echoes in his ears like a malediction. He feels the door yield, all that stands between him and providence giving way without resistance. How trusting the hand that turns the knob, admitting him sight unseen, and the night so black. In a heartbeat she stands before him. Eve, naked except for a silken chemise of a color he has no name for. She looks surprised to find him there, but not unduly so.

"I'll get a robe." Lightly, she closes the door.

When she returns her hair is combed back and a virginal velvet wrap obscures the curves of her hips and bosom. She smells of the spices that waft from the souk. Her skin retains a slight flush. She opens the door but doesn't invite him in, only stands to one side, studying his face.

"Are you all right?" she asks.

The messenger looks past her into the modest flat. He sees a wooden table covered with a crocheted cloth and adorned with a vase of crocuses. At one place setting, a teacup. Beside it, an empty bottle of 100-proof arak.

"I couldn't sleep," he says.

She hesitates a moment before responding, "A cup of tea sometimes helps."

She walks ahead into the kitchen and motions him toward a seat.

"Chamomile...peppermint...rosehip," her voice drifts back. While she gets down the teapot and lights the stove, he scans the contents of the shelves: more crocuses, a pepper mill, transparent glass canisters holding rice, oatmeal, lentils. He notes that she's left the door ajar.

"Bit of a draft." He retraces his steps and draws it closed.

As he crosses the room, he notes the small fireplace in the far corner and the rusty poker that leans against its grating. He's read in the tabloids about people getting bludgeoned to death with household objects: meat mallets, monkey wrenches, bowling trophies. Mentally, he paces off the distance between his chair and the poker's downturned handle.

"Do you take honey?" Eve asks.

"I've never liked sweet things."

She pulls the robe tight before placing the teapot on the table.

"Would you like something to eat?"

She stands beside him, more vulnerable than she knows, and inventories aloud the contents of her icebox. The messenger would like to warn her about the evil in the world, about Satan and the poison he injects into men's hearts, but he doesn't know how to begin. He has never been a patient man. Eve's naïveté precludes brevity. His eyes scan what he can see of her kitchen counter, searching for a knife.

She drops soundlessly into the chair beside him.

"How did you know where I live?"

"The Hungarian," he answers without thinking. "Old codger follows you around like a shadow."

A look of uneasiness crosses her face.

"A lot of lonely people find their way to Jerusalem."

The messenger, eyes skimming past her delicate cheekbones and the graceful slope of her neck, doesn't respond. Seeing no knife, his mind drifts again to the poker. He wonders how many blows it takes to clobber the life from a person, how much strength is required to crack open a skull.

"Have you no family here?" she asks.

"No—no one." Then, as an afterthought, "M'wife and kids back in Perth."

"You must miss them."

How to explain to this bleeding heart that he's come on a mission, and that all the rest—family, home, food, drink—has ceased to matter. What difference does it make if the mortgage is paid or the parsnips harvested? In the end God's wrath will make ashes of the world.

Eve inclines toward him and murmurs, "But, you've not touched your tea."

It occurs to him that if she would only leave the room for a moment, he could get his hands on the poker. He might come up behind her on tiptoe, strike so quickly she would be spared the terror of watching its dirty fang descend upon her head. Perhaps one or two blows would be sufficient to stun her. There would be no risk of her crying out after that.

"Ay, this headache," he says, clutching his temples and waiting for her to offer him something for the pain.

"Why didn't you say something sooner?"

He watches her rise from the chair and, stifling a yawn, walk in the direction of the kitchen. On reflex he springs to his feet and staggers to the fireplace. Nine paces—one less than he'd estimated—puts him within arm's reach of the poker. He crouches. His gaze at the level of a child's, he glances back across the room and sees Eve frozen in the doorway with a glass of water in her hands, smaller, paler than a moment before.

The poker, as if dislodged by the intensity of her stare, crashes to the floor with a resounding clang.

Crouching lower, he remembers school bells, firecrackers, Lydia already sprouting breasts at ten, a time when the end would have seemed inconceivable, with everything quickening, so impossibly alive. Shifting his gaze, he notices a single ember still burning in the fireplace. He remembers thinking that God had to have been a bloke to create anything as pretty as girls. He remembers sunsets the color of Eve's chemise and so big they made him shiver.

"You're out of wood," he says. "If y' like, I'll bring you some tomorrow."

But he knows he won't, knows he's been away too long already. Longer than a working man has the right. As he prods the fire back to life he can hear his heart hammer, damn these gates! And watching Eve's reflection undulate in the flames, he dares to hope there might still be a way back.

A TIME FOR PEACE

Mozes Koenig remembers what he'd like to forget, forgets what he'd like to remember, and wonders where the years have gone and how this old man—whose eyes can no longer distinguish a raisin from a cockroach and who pees in a thin downward arc—came to take up residence within his skin.

His trusty Olivetti, nearly as old as he, has ceased to cast back his reflection. Dull, its peeling black enamel. Flat, the *donk-donk* of his arthritic fingers plying the rust-edged keys. Wriggling his thumbs to bolster circulation, he feeds a sheet of onionskin paper into the typewriter and taps out A *Time for Peace*, then spacing down begins.

Jerusalem was burning, her streets choked with soldiers and anti-riot tanks. Child armies massed at the fault line. Life merged with headline, mingling ink and blood in one murky tragedy no one wanted, or understood.

Chapter one, untitled. A little gaudy, perhaps, but attention-getting. Plausible, if one has the generosity to allow an author the benefit of the doubt. "Sequel or treason?" the critics will debate, pinning motives on him, asking, "Whose side is he on, anyway?"

Mozes has had his defense ready for a quarter century.

"The side of truth," he will answer.

That this book will be his last, he accepts. He is running out of words, out of time, with all of his experience suddenly so transparent he can see to its very heart. His life will end in Jerusalem. With his dying breath he will stagger to the Wailing Wall and offer up his soul to the memory of Gizella. Gizella, the carnate angel who wrote the tablet on love with her kisses and fresh-baked kreplach. Gizella, who once made him a happy man.

It is a winter of discontinuities, Mozes surmises, and something at once sinister and miraculous aches to happen. Sensible people stay away from the Old City. The air, too still, suffocating, punishes the eyes with residual traces of tear gas. Fewer tourists, more soldiers and soothsayers, cluster outside the gates. The illusion of order has begun to fracture like the splintered windshield of an Egged bus. For Mozes, a Hungarian Jew, survivor of pogroms, world wars, genocide, and intellectual terrorism, Jerusalem can only truly become home once all predictability has fled.

Pulling the woolen bed cap from his head, he coaxes his frame into a sitting position, legs splayed between the muslin sheets like weather-beaten two-by-fours. Glare and chill intrude through the room's only windowpane. He fumbles on the commode for his spectacles. A pigeon perches for a moment on the outside ledge and cocks its head at him as if to ask, *nu?* Well?

"Who's complaining?" he says to the bird, reminding himself to leave a crust of bread on the sill.

He thinks about breakfast, pictures warm croissants slathered thick with butter and orange marmalade, then remembers his diet, a last-ditch attempt to reconstruct the physique that once earned him the nickname *Lombrago*, or one who chews foliage. The War left him with a hunger nothing could sate. Once the shortages ended, he discovered Viennese pastries, the fleeting oblivion of whipped cream and flaked chocolate, of marzipan and excess. His midsection has grown voluminous with the years, spilling over the waistband of his trousers like a giant cream puff.

He dresses hurriedly, daubs the tips of his mustache with Whisker wax, and smoothes his remaining hair into place. The bathroom mirror casts back the image of a bearish man: broad face, bushy brows, square symmetrical features. His oversized hands have the look of paws, hairy and thick-fingered. Lately, they have begun to fumble, overturning teacups, marking wrong numbers. He opens the medicine cabinet, reaches for the bottle of aftershave, only to watch it shatter against the tile floor.

"Clumsy oaf," he scolds himself and sweeps the shards into a corner with the toilet brush.

Grabbing his cashmere scarf from a peg on the wall, he heads for the front door, noting en route that his socks don't match and his loafers need polishing. Cursing under his breath in a combination of Yiddish and Hungarian, he gets down a tin of saddle soap and sets to work. Ten minutes later he closes the door behind him, descends the stairs, and steps into the street, light on his feet for a man of his girth and moving at a steady clip over the rutted sidewalks and uneven cobblestones.

At the corner of Jaffa Road he rests his elbows on the counter of a falafel stand and orders a cup of black coffee, then a second. Fortified, he heads south, skirting the Old City walls as far as Damascus Gate. He enters the souk. In the dim light, one face resembles another; he can't tell a lemon from a canary, a scroll from a rolling pin. The talismans, the brass urns, the embroidered robes and hand-loomed rugs…run together like splotches of paint on an artist's palette. A sea of bodies surrounds him, growing denser. The slimy nose of a donkey nuzzles the back of his hand. Entrails adhere to the soles of his shoes. The crowd gains force, siphoning the air from his lungs, pressing him deeper and deeper into the souk…the amulets, the heaped spices, the pyramids of oranges and pears, blurring, taking on the shapes of lost continents, of toppled cities.

He remembers Pest after the War, the rubble and the hunger. The flat he had lived in with Gizella and their twin sons empty, robbed of everything but a memorial candle, as if his wife's death had been foretold. Lost in time, he stumbles forward. He tastes tears. Europe lies in ruins, the Promised Land perishes beneath a holocaust of stones, no Jew spared. Gasping for breath, he catches hold of a door handle and braces against it.

"You've gone too far, grandfather," calls a young merchant, pointing with his chin toward a nearby alleyway. "She hasn't come out yet," he adds.

Mozes feels his face redden.

With feigned nonchalance, he calls back, "Just taking a stroll."

Lowering his chin into his collar, he maneuvers through the crowd and turns onto the residential side street—as familiar to him now as his own—with the wrought-iron balconies.

In front of the pocked and peeling facade of number 33 Saffron Street, he pauses and glances up. The gauze curtain, parted slightly, billows in the breeze. Behind it he glimpses the kinetic form of a woman's body, moving to the rhythm of a jazz ballad whose words he has forgotten.

Mozes dissembles his vigil by pretending to read the graffiti scrawled on a nearby wall. The writing is in Arabic, impossible to decipher. A half-dead dog lifts a shaky leg and urinates along its lower reaches. Mozes looks away. His foot begins to keep time with the music. He watches the dancing woman for as long as discretion permits, then bundling the scarf about his neck continues along the street, humming the tune.

What was it, Mozes never ceased to wonder, that drew him back day after day to Saffron Street? The dark fire in a lonely woman's eyes? The magnetism of her lithe body? He can't say. He only knows he needs a heroine, that flesh-and-blood someone whose passion can jar free the words held hostage in his imagination. The streets of Jerusalem, for so many writers an inexhaustible mine of odes and epics, inspire in him nothing but lethargy. He needs this woman who dances alone behind a gauze curtain. He needs her youth, her tragic face, her contradictions...her sad and solitary dance that *is* Jerusalem, that lets him know he belongs here if only to tell her story.

He first came to Israel five years before glasnost—illegally—driven by some vague notion of reunion, of finding in the footsteps of his biblical namesake a reason to go on coaxing his osteoporitic bones out of bed each morning. Gizella, gifted with senses that defied time and distance, had enthralled him with her vision of a land lifted from the pages of the Torah. She described the gossamer quality of the light, the moonlike austerity of the Judean hills, the riotous glut of the souks with their intermingling scents of mint and roasted sesame.

"I see you there," she had told him, her ebony eyes wide with prophecy. "You're old, you pose questions to every saint and madman but are too distracted to listen for an answer." She had patted his hand then, he remembers, to reassure him. "Just as well, *boubala*. What matters is to keep asking the questions."

Nothing—and yet, everything—had been as Gizella described it.

Rendered gypsy by thwarted dreams, he drifted from Tel Aviv to the Negev Desert, from Beersheba to Haifa, from Kibbutz Degania to the inevitable—Jerusalem. He had expected the fabled landscape to soothe him, to give him back the vital pieces of himself that age and loss had stolen, but instead he stepped through Jaffa Gate and realized with a shudder that Jerusalem was a city entirely made of stone.

His Olivetti sat idle. Doubting everything he once believed, doubting even his doubts, he listened to the jackals howl articles of faith at one another and sat hunched like an empty sack over the keyboard. How many thousands of times did he crank a sheet of onionskin paper into the carriage only to sit staring over its edge through the cracked windowpane, watching cats slink along the ramparts and soldiers pace tight-jawed at their posts. One more itinerant writer picking through the wreckage of the Jewish experience for a measly sliver of truth.

But today, Mozes feels inspired. As he approaches the faithful old typewriter that has become his nemesis, he can almost feel affection for its decrepitude.

"Be nice, and I might treat you to an oiling," he bargains with the machine, giving the keys a quick dusting off with his handkerchief.

Humming, he sits down at his desk. His fingers poise on the keyboard, caress the rusty places, prime the pump...even as his mind goes blank—blank like the unused ream of paper that has lain yellowing at his fingertips for as long as he can remember. Crestfallen, he pads to the bookcase and takes down a hardcover book. Holding the weighty tome in both hands, he stares with a curious lack of satisfaction at his name on the dust jacket. The book's title, A Time for War, provokes a sensation akin to nausea.

Nearly four decades before, when he wrote this protracted battle cry, he had all the answers. The book was fired by the conviction— brutish to him now—that only the taking up of arms could restore Jewish virility. The message was nowhere as well received as in Israel, where a warrior culture was already taking hold. The Hebrew translation of A Time for War recently entered its tenth edition. Elsewhere the book has been out of print since the demise of the crewcut. In Budapest or New York, no one has heard of Mozes Koenig; in Tel Aviv he is a living legend. It doesn't matter that he has not written another book since the dubious success of his first—or rather has not completed one, for he's begun dozens. Nor does it make the least bit of difference that he's ceased to believe a word of his own magnum opus. The royalty checks arrive just the same. Scaled down a digit, it's true, since he abdicated the role of honorary spokesman for the Israeli army, but providing a modest income.

Mozes, much to his publisher's chagrin, has no stomach for violence anymore. Even the morning headlines unsettle his digestion.

When a man can no longer distinguish his memories from his night terrors, he reasons, what's the use of continuing to fight? If he could, he would take every Israeli schoolboy on his knee and tell him, "Enough already. Enough."

But it's to his own sons, grown men now, that he will dedicate his sequel.

His twin boys were born in the wrong place at the wrong time—Budapest, 1939—and although Mozes couldn't have known it then, they were born to break his heart. Hungary's Jews were disappearing—some into hiding, some herded off to fates he could envision only in nightmares, still others murdered before his eyes. At Gizella's urging he took the tots from their cribs one foggy morning in '42, swaddled them in a horsehair blanket along with a last loaf of bread, and carried them into the countryside near Tatabanya. Seeing a pair of fair-haired peasant boys picking through the frozen soil for the last of their family's crop of sugar beets, he paused to watch them. The lads were thin but hardy. Their faces held no sign of want.

With the twins growing heavier and heavier in his arms, he followed the boys home. Their house was a simple wooden cottage. Through a narrow half-shuttered window he could see a fire burning in the hearth. Mozes ascended the doorstep. As he placed his sons before the broad unplaned door, he heard footsteps on the other side, then a hand on the latch. Chest thundering, he drew his Luger.

For a moment the sight of the peasant woman's face mottled with fear, her chapped hands and the moth-eaten apron she wore, sapped his resolve—but only for a moment. Thrusting open the door, he lunged into the house, holding the gun at arm's length in front of him, cocked, aimed to kill, and as steady as his emotional state allowed.

"If my sons die, your sons die," he told her.

The words shot out like the bullets he didn't have; the Luger's breech was empty.

An old man emerged from the back room and, inching forward on withered legs, shook a finger at him, as if administering a scolding to a naughty child.

"Put that thing away," he sputtered, "before you hurt someone."

Mozes lowered the gun. The man limped toward an unvarnished table. Seating himself with a low moan, he prompted the woman, "You've not offered our guest a cup of tea," and apologized for his daughter's lapse of hospitality.

Mozes backed sheepishly out the front door and returned with the twins, who had begun to cry from cold and hunger.

"Poor little *babas*," murmured the old Magyar.

The daughter fed them each a small bowl of cabbage broth fortified with pigs' feet, carefully conserving the pork scraps. Mozes watched his sons' faces grow placid. Feeling his own composure erode by degrees, he hurriedly drained the teacup and rose to excuse himself.

As he set off down the front path, the peasant woman cried after him, "What shall we call them?"

"Try Geza and Imre," he told her, good gentile names.

Two years, nine months and twenty-one days would elapse before he returned to fetch his sons. By that time they had grown into these makeshift aliases, and who was he to tell them they weren't what they thought they were but two displaced Jews named David and Itzik?

Mozes took them home to an empty debris-strewn apartment where no mother waited—while he served as a Partisan, Gizella had been gunned down by Nazis en route to Dachau, a corpse at twenty-one. Though he was not more than a living corpse, he tried to give David and Itzik a childhood, but it was no use. Their little lips curled in skepticism each time he'd reach for the volume of Mother Goose.

Gizella's homilies and lullabies still whispered to him from the wood-work, but his sons hadn't the ears to hear them. Even in his lifetime they had become orphans.

Defiant, Mozes opens the refrigerator door and takes out a jar of marmalade, a tub of butter, and a pitcher of heavy cream. From the bread box he extracts the last of the croissants and the end piece from a loaf of pumpernickel bread. Tucking a dishcloth into the neck of his nightshirt, he eats leaning against the countertop. When only a crust of bread remains, he prepares himself a pot of rosehip tea and gravitates, cup and saucer in hand, toward the typewriter.

Pounding at the keys with bared-tooth ferocity, he types, *Through the shadow of Jaffa Gate emerged a woman, lighting up the old stones like a nova streaming across the night sky. A woman with the heart of a water bearer. A woman so tragic she could only be called...Eve.* The heroine who eluded him all those years. Where has she been hiding, ripening, while he grows old for want of inspiration? Perhaps she has dropped some clue, but Mozes can't remember. Her age, he hasn't asked, being too much of a gentleman and preferring to invent her. He decides she must be thirty or so. That golden moment when a woman still has youth if not innocence, and her passion pours itself onto the page like plum liqueur lavishing a crepe suzette.

Mozes reaches absently for his teacup. The tea is cold, not sweet enough. He thinks about lunch but can't generate sufficient enthu-siasm to lift his mass out of the desk chair and scavenge the sparse contents of his refrigerator a second time.

On an impulse he reaches into a bottom drawer and rifles through the letters, postcards, and bric-a-brac until he finds what he's looking for. A worn, sepia-colored photograph. On the back, written in faded red ink, *Gizella, 1938.*

He studies the small dear face. The eyes, it's true, are dark like Eve's, the cheekbones high, but there any obvious resemblance ends. Gizella, even before the War, had the skittish look of a doe. Mozes remembers how the click of the camera's shutter had made her start, softly blurring her finely chiseled features, rendering the image as enigmatic and off-center as his recollection of her. He takes another long look at the photograph, then he replaces it and closes the drawer.

Eve resembles Gizella to the extent that stars seen from a distance seem to emit the same light or faces glimpsed through the fogged window of a passing tram might be variations on one face. Muttering to himself, he reopens the drawer. Again he studies the photograph.

"I could have sworn...the eyes, dark as hazelnuts...the way they never quite smile...but no, no, Gizella was more fragile. My poor Gizi, you weren't made for this world."

He remembers the combed cotton nightdress she would wear, mauve-colored with butterflies embroidered on the bodice. He remembers how she would rise from bed—regardless of the hour—and fix him a plate of leftover flanken with horseradish or warmed-over sweet rolls filled with strawberry jam. Their bedroom would be chilly, but the kitchen stayed warm. They would sit close to each other, occupying the same chair, not needing to speak. Sometimes she would braid her hair...such beautiful hair. The Nazis would have shaved her head, like they did to his cousin Ferenc. Ferenc's hair never grew back. He took to wearing a black fedora after the War; its brim cast a permanent shadow across his face. His one surviving son insisted on burying the bald man bare-headed, which seemed to Mozes a final indignity.

Stifling a sigh, he clears the desktop of memories and pads into the bedroom to dress. The day has passed without his having noticed.

Achy in the joints, he eases into a starched oxford shirt and pressed gabardine pants and draws a hairbrush across his pate. Having forgotten to buy a bottle of aftershave to replace the one he broke the morning before, he splashes a bit of mouthwash onto his jowls, then thinking better of it rinses his face with tap water.

Pulling on his scarf, he descends the stairs. The street—already dark—lies deserted, except for a scavenging dog with a swath of flypaper adhering to its flanks.

"Bad day, my friend?" Mozes says to the mutt.

A sufferer of night blindness, Mozes pauses to get his bearings. He used to navigate by counting streetlamps, until the route to Saffron Street became imprinted in his cells, a zigzagging walk through the souk and across the Via Dolorosa, down the fetid rows of butcher shops to the saving havoc of spice stalls.

Fixing his gaze on the large unshuttered window, Mozes feels his heartbeat quicken. He can hear music, something rhythmic and primitive played at low volume. On the far side of the gauze curtain a candle glows, hinting at, rather than illuminating, a four-poster bed piled high with white pillows. Straining his eyes, he discerns the silhouette of a woman prone atop the white sheets. No clothing dissembles the perilous curve of her hips, the abandon with which she extends her arms above her head, accentuating the seismic rise and fall of her breasts. As Mozes watches, Eve sits up and runs a hand though her unruly black hair. A moment later a second figure enters the tableau—a man. His hand reaches toward a switch. Light floods the room, exposing their nakedness in all its beauty and derangement. Eve rises to her knees and begins to sway to the music, to sway with arms upstretched and thighs thrust forward and legions of dragonflies tracing frantic circles at her window.

Mozes turns away and braces against a crumbling door frame. Nothing feels solid. The music stops, and he can hear the man's soft groans. Then his voice, shrieking in whispers, "My angel, my *houri*, mine!"

Mozes lies sleepless in his narrow bed, aware of termites eating away the foundations of his apartment block and the night caving in. He feels skinless. The woolen blanket weighs on him like a slab of granite.

The nights have been like this—black holes—since he lost Gizella. While she shared his pillow, he had only to lie beside her to feel his heart swell like a loaf of bread rising in the oven.

His father had been a baker. Tired-eyed and uncomplaining, he'd wrench himself from bed each morning before first light so that the people of Derzs might have fresh poppyseed rolls and challah for breakfast. That Mozes would one day be a scholar, the faithful baker never doubted. By the time the boy was seven he had read the Talmud, by ten the Kaballah. Mozes read with his tummy full and the aroma of baking bread assuring him his world was whole. However hard the Torah sages might try to plant dark intimations in the unscathed matter of his soul, he slept soundly.

What would he not give now for a slice of his father's bread, to hear a loving voice call him *zunchikal*, my little son. To wake from a night's rest and have someone ask, "What did you dream?"

The War cut short his youth. He wasn't yet nineteen when the Partisan recruiter—a hunchback known only as Fox—issued him his first Luger, still warm from the hand of a dead Nazi soldier. The feel of it, strange and mighty, aroused his still-adolescent body like the sight of a big-bosomed woman.

Fox showed him the basics: where to load the bullets, how to pull the trigger.

"It's like copulating," the Partisan said, handing him the gun barrel-first. "No one has to teach you how to shoot; when the time is right, you just know." Mozes nodded to dissemble his apprehension and stuck the pistol in the waistband of his trousers, which had grown roomy since the food shortages.

For months he kept the weapon hidden—first in the cookie jar, then the coal bin, and finally beneath his pillow, where it drained all color from his dreams. Nights lost definition. Gizella would awaken at odd hours, clutching at his shoulders, murmuring, "It won't be long now."

There were no more dawns, only floods of glare, cutting through the clouds like hellfire.

"It won't be long," she would whisper, shielding his eyes with the long dark train of her hair.

Once he'd carried his sons to safety and made his peace with his wife, who would not be convinced to flee the country without the twins, he set out on his first mission alongside the mysterious Fox. At the Yugoslav border they joined a motley contingent of fighters, dispossessed Jews like himself—students, merchants, and tailors who had never fired a gun. Because Mozes was the greenest of the lot and not yet as threadbare or hungry as they, Fox adopted him as his protégé. While the others set up a makeshift camp in the countryside outside Szeged, they entered the city, lurching from shadow to shadow, pausing in doorways to listen for the rumble of tanks or the smug squeak of German boots. At a ramshackle warehouse on the fringe of the industrial district they synchronized their watches and separated, and Mozes ventured toward the city center to scavenge for food.

An eerie silence blanketed the streets. People clung to the illusory safety of four walls and a lock on the door, except for those unfortunate souls hungry enough to risk their lives in pursuit of a wormy head of cabbage or a starved hen.

He had not gone far when he heard a woman—frantic, judging

by the pitch of her voice—cry out for help. The gunmetal burned at his waist. Clumsily, without cover, he turned a corner and found himself face to face with an S.S. officer.

The German, too drunk to be startled, almost smiled. A young woman, as pillaged as her empty shopping bag, broke free from his arms. Shattering the silence, she threw back her head and whinnied, her face a bloody pulp.

There was no struggle. In a split second Mozes' hand had gone for the pistol and fired point blank, killing the officer on the spot.

Had the young Partisan walked away then, leaving the dead German to settle accounts with his Maker, today he might be an innocent man. But he couldn't. As if some primal instinct resurrected from an earlier evolution had seized control of his limbs, he kicked the cadaver in the teeth. Once. Twice...he didn't keep count. He was thinking of his sons growing up among strangers who fed on the flesh of pigs, of Gizella adrift in a world that hated the pure of heart.

At some point the Nazi's face had to have come apart and oozed onto his boot, but Mozes doesn't remember. It has taken him fully half a century to reconstruct even the broad outline.

After Ferenc's funeral while Mozes sat alone in his flat drinking Tokaji, the defaced Nazi had come back to haunt him. Not unkindly, though the mere sight of him was enough to rend a vault. Having cohabited with a succession of ghosts since the War, Mozes merely refilled his glass and asked the visitor what he wanted.

"To rest," the apparition told him through the cavity where his face had once been. "Stop pounding your chest, old man, and let me be."

Mozes, curiously sober, pulled on a trench coat over his flannel nightshirt and strode through the snowy streets of Budapest's seventh district to the Chain Bridge. The night was moonless. Mozes had forgotten how many stars a sky could hold. With eyes fixed on Orion, he hurled his vintage Luger into the Danube.

Morning finds Mozes planted once again beneath Eve's window, mustache freshly waxed, a bouquet of crocuses clasped against his belly. Doors creak open, slam closed. Housewives sweep dust and rat droppings out onto the street. The wind carries the refuse west, along with the bittersweet memory of lemon trees.

"Here so early, grandfather?" says the young merchant, as he saunters by in shiny black pants and a yellow jersey.

"Morning constitutional."

The young man winks an eye.

"Beautiful flowers," he smirks, glancing up at Eve's balcony. "She will like them."

Mozes pretends not to have heard the remark. He comments on the return of the raptors, then points south, tracking the flight of a vulture with his upraised index finger. He hasn't slept. His hands feel as heavy as lead paperweights. Yawning, he sits down on the curb and his arms sink forward onto his knees. The crocuses tumble unnoticed into the gutter.

The door of number 33 swings open and Eve emerges, walking past him as if he were invisible. Unnerved by her abrupt and unexpected appearance, he can only stare after her.

She wears a simple unstructured dress. Its color reminds Mozes of the wild raspberries he and Gizella would gather along the banks of Lake Balaton. Her hair is pulled back in a loose braid and large silver earrings dangle to the hollow of her neck. As she turns the corner, he collects himself and trails behind, cursing his girth and the fashionable new loafers that pinch his toes.

There are more shadows than people in the souk. Keeping Eve

squarely in his field of vision, he treads on tiptoe down the cavernous Via Dolorosa onto David Street, where the more dogged merchants tend shuttered shops between rounds of backgammon and dominoes. Eve glides past them, her footfalls soundless, silver earrings swaying to a rhythm only she can hear. Slowing pace, she turns down Christian Quarter Road. Mozes follows. He has begun to tire and his sides ache.

It isn't the first time a plot has outdistanced him, left him creeping like a blind mouse through a maze. At such times he consoles himself that there are worse things than to die a one-book author. But when he's honest with himself, the thought of leaving behind nothing but his tales of desperate men committing desperate acts fills him with a profound sense of failure. He longs to set things right. If only he could call out Eve's name, take her aside, beg her to tell him how the story ends.

As if hearing his thoughts, she pauses. The wind lifts the braid from her back and lightly sets it down again. Nothing else moves. She gazes up at the sky, down at the stones, then slowly turns to face him.

"You've been following me," she says. "Why?"

Mozes hedges. "I thought you might enjoy some company."

He knows she doesn't believe him, knows she understands the impulses that drive people to recklessness and worse, knows she has too good a heart to call an old man a liar.

When she doesn't respond, he ventures, "Might we pick up the thread?" then fearing he has overstepped, stammers, "Walking alone like this, it isn't safe."

He would like to tell her how it was to go back to his flat after the War, to sit alone in the empty rooms and hear his neighbor's tone-deaf daughter practice scales on what had been Gizella's piano, to see his wife's favorite dress—the dress she had worn on their wedding day—hanging like a shroud on the graceless body of the concierge. He'd like to hold Eve's dove-like hands to his heart and say, I've come so far yet understand so little.

The wind shifts direction. Cypresses flutter their boughs in a timeless salute to the sun. Mozes watches the raptors reclaim their kingdom of air, watches his past drift from sight like a cloud on the wind. The day feels newborn. Eve's gaze rests like a sunbeam on his tired face.

"We were never strangers," she says, closing the distance between them with her glimmer of a smile, closing the distance, taking him by the hand.

Certain that he's died in his sleep, Mozes lies flat in bed with arms crossed atop his chest. He wonders what's become of his aches and pains, and why he's never noticed the brightly painted shutters on his neighbor's house.

"I've become a ghost," he says to himself, palpating his limbs.

This body feels not quite his but substantial, undeniably alive. Comforted, he wriggles his toes. He shall like being a ghost, he decides, rolling languidly onto his side and continuing to dawdle.

At noon he slips barefoot from bed, pads yawning into the living room, and finds a stack of manuscript pages piled beside his Olivetti—a stack so high he can read its cover page without putting on his spectacles. Humming softly to himself, he leafs through the sheets of onionskin paper. As he nears bottom, his eyes fix on a passage: *The day will come when there will be no more tanks, no crust of blood on the old stones. Then Eve will descend from her tower and dance before God and man, and her dance will bring back the dead children, the lost gardens, the songbirds...*

Mozes no longer hears his own voice. With the words sweet on his lips, he rises and stung with grace begins to pirouette through the musty flat. The first star breaks through, the story ends, yet Mozes keeps on dancing. He hums a rhapsody whose lyrics elude memory, and feels Gizella—Gizi, his tender bride—snug within his embrace.

IMAGING EVE

mal Mahmoud lives in a house that refuses to fall down
though a thousand deaths weigh upon it. There's the blood
stain on the roof from the cat that got shelled during the
War of '67. There's the portrait of the disgraced great-uncle assassi-
nated for getting too friendly with Ben-Gurion. There are the bullet
holes from when the masked *fedaye* ambushed the British soldier.
The rooms stay dark all day long. Amal dreams every night about the
house toppling over, but in the morning she finds it still standing.
She dreams that a man lifts her from the debris and carries her out
into the light, but no man comes.

Things have not gone well for the Mahmouds since the Israelis
got greedy and annexed East Jerusalem. Amal's uncles and cousins
have left the city, seeking their fortune in Germany or the Gulf. Her
favorites still send photographs of skyscrapers and newborn babies to
let her know that life goes on. But she wonders. East Jerusalem
doesn't change, it just grows dingier. How can the future happen
with so much history clinging to the stones?

Since her father stopped working and her mother let the maid
go, Amal has assumed by default the task of cleaning the house.
Having been raised for a very different life, she feels a visceral distaste for household implements and the noxious pine cleanser with
which she douses every fixture and floorboard. The rooms seem to
multiply as she works. There is always one more to mop or dust, one
more endless expanse of lusterless parquet…and the days getting
shorter.

The house has become a repository of family memorabilia dating
back to the seventh century when the first Mahmouds, sheiks and
caliphs to a man, brought the one true religion to the babel that was

Jerusalem. There is too much of everything—carpets atop carpets, tables beside tables, urns and swords and hookahs spilling into the corridors. Amal must walk sideways. A ring of keys jangles at her waist. There are more locks than keys, closets whose contents remain hidden to her, thresholds she has never crossed. Her Aunt Sana says that the family patriarchs kept their various wives sequestered in separate quarters, each overseen by a eunuch. Amal wonders what became of the eunuchs' testicles, and if she would recognize one if she found it. Perhaps they were buried in the basement, along with the tiny bodies of the discarded baby girls Aunt Sana is forever mourning.

Amal begins each day's labors in her brother's bedchamber, where the scent of Eau Sauvage lingers long after Salim has dressed and left for work. The room holds thirteen gilt-framed mirrors—Amal has counted them. Each time she aims her spray bottle at the glass, she confronts the image of a plain grown girl, not quite a woman, with a face more serious than pretty and breasts that get lost in her proper white blouse.

Salim got the looks in the family, inherited from their mother, who used to be mistaken for the American movie actress who brought Tarzan down from the trees. Aunt Sana calls Salim a gigolo, the way he spends his paycheck on clothes and prances around the big hotels. But Amal, trusting that Allah bestows on the faithful precisely the face each deserves, believes that her brother's handsomeness must reflect his superior virtue.

Salim, never having been expected to pick up after himself, leaves his day-old clothes strewn across the Turkish rugs. Amal sometimes finds empty beer bottles or foil-wrapped condoms beneath his bed. Once, she found a magazine with naked women in it. The magazine was in English. Some of the women wore little white tails as if they were rabbits. Aunt Sana says that men make sex objects out of women because secretly they're afraid of them, an assertion Amal has as little reason to believe as to disbelieve. She doesn't presume to understand Salim. How he feels when he looks at these dirty women with their private parts displayed like overpriced melons is not for a sister to know.

And yet, how not to wonder about her only brother?

Six years her senior, Salim has the freedom to come and go as he pleases. In recent months he has come home only to sleep. His meals he takes on the street or not at all. Late at night she sometimes hears him tiptoe up the staircase and run a bath. Mornings he emerges puffy-eyed from his bedroom, drinks a cup of coffee with three sugars, and, racing down the overgrown path to his parked Datsun, calls over a shoulder to her, "How much do you charge for a smile?"

That her brother leads an interesting life full of social engage-ments and *affaires de coeur*, Amal has no doubt. His movie star looks, his charm, the way his jaw dimples when he smiles—a woman would have to be made of dough not to be slayed by these things. Aunt Sana says you can't trust a man whose pants hold a crease, but when Amal dreams of a secret sweetheart, she pictures him sleek and fine just like Salim.

Amal plumps her brother's pillow and tucks in his bedsheet. She runs a dustcloth across the top of his bureau, pausing to leaf through a slim volume of verse she's never seen there before—Kabir, some raving heretic whose name she recognizes from a list of banned books.

Salim, an aficionado of poetry? The contents of his one small bookcase would hardly suggest so. Amal's cloth skims along the bind-ings of mysteries by Agatha Christie and Arthur Conan Doyle, biog-raphies of Prince Rainier, King Hussein, and the Shah of Iran, a guidebook to Provence, a German-Arabic dictionary, and an intro-duction to stamp collecting.

Her curiosity piqued, she opens the top drawer of Salim's bureau and rifles through a chaos of handkerchiefs, cufflinks, breath mints, socks, pens, and playing cards. She crosses to his desk and begins to examine, scrap by scrap, the meager contents of the litter basket. The chewing gum wrappers she discards without interest. She glances at a tag from a pair of imported Sergio Valente bluejeans, a torn-in-half receipt from the new unisex hair salon on Salah-ah-Din Street, a lottery ticket. Squatting, she studies a note Salim has written to himself on lined newsprint torn from a spiral notebook—a reminder to change the car oil—and beneath it, in lipstick-red ink, a name and telephone number: *Eve Cavell, 71700.*

Satisfied, Amal pockets the slip of paper.

Some days Amal imagines Eve haughty and wicked, the sort of woman whose Salomeic body and painted lips force men to sin in their hearts just by looking at her. Other days she can almost feel sorry for her. She imagines Eve love-lost in a rented flat, pictures her waiting at the window for Salim, perfumed for him, the time passing slowly, slowly. And Salim late, no doubt.

Amal has never had a beau much less a lover, but she knows that love can tear pieces from a woman. She has read the forbidden books. She's heard her mother cry at night when her father drinks too much arak and starts breaking things.

Her brother Salim does his drinking out. Matchbooks collect beside his bed: the American Colony Hotel, the Inter-Continental, the Hilton…She smells these places on Salim's soiled shirts, the cigarette smoke and imported cognac. Eve she smells in his pants. Aunt Sana has explained to her that Muslim men do with foreign women what they wouldn't dare do with their own—and that foreign women come to East Jerusalem to fornicate because everyone knows that

Arab men make the most passionate lovers. Amal wonders if Eve has fornicated with other men before her brother. She wonders what endearments Eve whispers to Salim while she submits to such shameful acts, and how she can face her neighbors the morning after. Distracted, she fails to notice her mother observing her from the doorway.

"Always dreaming, my Amal," the matron says with a wistful smile. "Leave that for now and come downstairs. Your father has a visitor. A scholar."

Another second-rate academic wanting to hear about the Mahmouds' lost glory, Amal thinks, laying aside the laundry basket without the least relish.

"Rub lotion on your hands," her mother directs, "and comb your hair. You'll serve tea, the Earl Grey."

"Is *waalid* well?"

"Your father hasn't had more than one or two drinks," her mother responds in a whisper, drawing the door closed behind her. "His nerves are on edge—whose aren't?—with the curfews and strikes and everyone giving orders. Once things return to normal, I will speak to him about going to work for my brother Fuad." She fingers the pearls at her neck and smoothes the silken bodice of her once-chic black dress. "We've run out of glacéed chestnuts—remind me to ask your uncle to send another tin. Our guest looks like a man who appreciates sweets."

"There's baklava."

"But that's so common."

She takes a step forward and inspects her daughter at closer range.

"Your hands, how coarse they look."

Amal tries to picture her mother dressed in a brightly colored sarong, swinging through tree boughs in the arms of a well-muscled ape man, but the matriarch's bearing won't soften to the role. Her expensively shod feet refuse to leave the ground.

"Once things return to normal, we shall see about making you presentable."

Amal says nothing, only tucks her hands behind the scratchy muslin of her apron and again conjures up the ape man, dangling from the chandelier, poised to carry her mother off with one mighty swipe of his hairy arms.

That the visitor is a Jew, Amal quickly surmises from her father's exaggerated politeness and thinly veiled contempt. The two men sit elbow to elbow on a low overstuffed sofa that once belonged to a Turkish pasha, both puffing on Havana cigars. Her father has taken his silk smoking jacket out of mothballs and slicked his hair back with tonic. He speaks his best Oxford English. Her mother perches on a throne-like seat at the far corner of the room. She wears a beatific expression and holds herself very erect, breaking her silence only to ask, "More tea?"

Her father introduces the visitor as Dr. Koenig, a professor of Middle East Studies from Budapest, Hungary.

The old scholar, portly and stiff-jointed, rises with difficulty and bows from the waist. His lips pucker, as if he intends to kiss her hand, but she doesn't extend it. Each time he catches Amal's eye he winks at her, causing his waxed mustache to tilt at unlikely angles.

As she refills his teacup, he asks in academic-sounding Arabic, "Why so serious, little one?"

Before she can reply, her father extinguishes his cigar and says tersely, "And how would you have her comport herself, Herr Professor? If she does not smile, it is because she has no birthright, no future. She was born too late."

# # #

Amal peers over the back gate, waiting to see the visitor exit the house. She stands in the shade of the one surviving orange tree, inhaling the perfume of its blossoms, thinking, this is what Palestine once smelled like. The neighbor's maid hangs laundry on a line, satin bedsheets and French lingerie, the sort of things her father used to bring back from Saudi Arabia the years he worked there. The gardener plants bulbs. As Amal watches the clods of earth yield beneath his spade, she hears the front door open and close and knows that the visitor has left.

A moment later his stout figure appears on the untended walkway leading to the street. He wears too much clothing for the season, as if he were still dressing for the nippy autumns of Budapest. Amal's mother races down the path to hand him his umbrella. He reaches toward his head as if to tip his hat to her, only he isn't wearing one.

"How very kind," she hears him say in his funny accent.

Amal turns, intending to reenter the house. She watches the Hungarian step off the curb and gaze about in all directions, by all appearances lost. On an impulse she opens the gate and sprints toward him.

"Is that you, little one?" He smiles broadly.

Amal, glancing nervously toward the house, hastens to say, "I can't stay long."

They take a few steps in the direction of the Old City, the professor humming, Amal watching their shadows sprawl slantwise across the paving stones.

"I have a confession," he says suddenly, turning to face her. "I'm an impostor, a fraud. Not a scholar at all, but a common busybody. I write books any simpleton can understand."

armored truck and take up positions beside a shwarma stand. A lame dog licks dust from their boots.

As she nears Damascus Gate, hawkers cry out their wares, donkeys bray, and an endless stream of strangers pours into the souk. Pressed inexorably forward by the crush of bodies, she staggers along the rows of shops and up and down the broken steps, emerging with a jolt at the end of David Street, where a blinding stab of sunlight marks the outer limit of her world.

With every nerve on alert she steers a course toward the Tower of David, then beyond it to Jewish Quarter Road. Gradually the route widens, giving onto a spacious courtyard rimmed by sidewalk cafés and souvenir shops. She is aware of jackhammers, of old things rendered new. The buildings wear recent facades, but Amal isn't fooled. She knows that Palestinians have shed blood here. She feels their fretful souls hover on the doorsteps.

Taking Dr. Koenig's calling card from her pocket, she studies the address and tries to match the cryptic Hebrew squiggles with the street signs she passes to left and right. She doesn't dare ask for directions. Soon all the squares and rows of flats begin to look alike, the faces look alike, even the clouds run together, and she no longer knows which way is forward, which way back.

"Ha'im halacht leh ibud?"

She turns to find a young curly-haired man in tweeds eying her with curiosity.

"Are you lost?" he repeats in English.

"No," she says timidly. Then, emboldened by the man's mild demeanor, "Well, maybe."

She holds out the professor's card, fidgeting with the buttons on her cardigan as he reads it aloud.

"Professor Mozes Koenig—he's our neighbor. That's his flat, over there." He points toward a modest old building with oversized windows. "I saw him go out a while ago."

She thanks him and begins to walk away.

"No need to run off like that," she hears him call after her. "Let me invite you for a cup of coffee. Dr. Koenig's bound to come back before long." He falls into step beside her. "There's a coffeehouse nearby. You'll be able to watch for him."

Amal pauses to look at the man's face, which is clean-shaven and softly rounded. His eyes, a placid gray-green, remind her of fennel seed.

"You'd be doing me a favor," he goes on. "I'm visiting with my family for a few days and I need a break."

He directs her toward a small corner café with wrought-iron tables and umbrellas that say Cinzano. Before she can protest, he pulls out a chair for her.

"Are you sure the professor will pass this way?" she asks.

"At his age, people don't alter course."

He steps up to a counter and orders two odd-smelling coffees with whipped cream on top.

"The professor doesn't get many visitors anymore." He takes a seat beside her. "My parents look in on him now and again—they worry that he'll asphyxiate in that little flat or die of loneliness." He sits back. The coffees' whipped cream peaks slowly deflate. "You're quiet. Is it shyness or am I talking too much?"

"I don't get out often," she replies.

"You don't study? I thought you might be a foreign student or a guest worker on a kibbutz. Habit I have, trying to place people."

Avoiding his eyes, she ventures, "My origins might surprise you."

Grinning, he inclines toward her.

"Don't tell me, let me guess. You're the illegitimate daughter of the Greek Patriarch. Or a defector from the Bolshoi Ballet. No, more likely you've been sent by aliens with a message that could save the planet. Am I right?"

Amal laughs despite the knot in her throat.

"I'm a runaway Cinderella from a neighboring galaxy."

"A neighboring galaxy?" he says with childlike merriment. "And where might that be?"

"East Jerusalem."

For a moment they stare off into the distance, he licking cream from his lips, she exuding defiance.

"That's cool," he says finally. He pushes aside his coffee and stretches out his legs, revealing a pair of well-worn Nikes. "I'm Doron Eliam." He inclines his head in greeting and the smile returns to his lips. "Didn't mean to make you feel uncomfortable. It's just that one doesn't see many Arabs—*Palestinians*, I mean—in the Jewish Quarter since the riots started."

"The *Intifada*, you mean."

He shrugs his shoulders.

"People call things by different names. I'm not political."

"But you're Israeli," she rejoins, determined to hold him accountable. "You must serve in the army."

"Not with an ulcer. I held a clerical position for a year or so, then they discharged me. Now I study business at Columbia University. It's not my thing, business, but in my family, you either sit behind a cash register or teach at Yeshiva. I just don't see myself with a beard." He pauses to chuckle at his own joke. "But tell me about you."

"What do you want to know?"

"The one thing you never told anyone."

Amal traces figure-eights on the tabletop with a jittery index finger.

"The one thing..." she repeats. "I could tell you that I have no secrets, but that would be a lie. I have nothing but secrets. No one asks me what I think about."

"*I'm* asking."

"Impossibilities," she whispers. "I think about what it would be like to burn my identity card and go anywhere I want, be anyone I want."

"You mean, freedom?"

"No, dignity. People call things by different names."

A girl soldier sidles past and takes her place at the next table. Amal watches in grim fascination as she fastens a Walkman to her head, turns up the volume, and begins to tap out a beat with the toe of her graceless combat boot.

"Can I get you another coffee?"

"I can't stay," Amal replies, glancing nervously at her companion's wristwatch. Then, noting his disappointment, she prefaces her leave-taking, "I'm glad to have met you, Doron Eliam."

"I'll be here for a few more days. Maybe you can come back another time. My family's sitting *shivah*, but they're used to my disappearances."

"*Shivah?*"

"It's the way Jews mourn their dead. A cousin of mine was killed in that fire bombing everyone's talking about. It's been in all the papers."

She removes the dark glasses from her eyes and studies his face.

"I'm sorry."

"It's not your fault. Some fanatic blows his stack, innocent people die—shall I blame every Palestinian for the actions of a few?"

"But, could you *love* a Palestinian?" She feels herself blush.

"One hears of cases…"

Silence comes between them like a wedge. Amal thinks, this could only have ended badly. Hurrying now, she replaces Salim's sunglasses and pushes back her chair.

"Hey, that was a cop-out." He takes a ballpoint pen from his breast pocket, scribbles his telephone number on a paper napkin, and places it before her. "What I meant to say is, first, people need to know each other. Look at us. We live in the same city, our families have lived here for generations, yet it's a small miracle that we've met at all."

"Yes, a miracle," she echoes, recording the young man's image in her memory, locking it deep inside even as she stands to go.

"You haven't told me your name."

"Amal," she says. "It means hope."

Amal closes the door of her brother's bedchamber and picks up the telephone. Nothing stirs in the house. Her father hasn't risen from bed in two days. Her mother has gone with Sana to pay a call on a rich relative visiting from Europe. Salim has left for work. From her apron pocket she takes a slip of paper, its red lettering faded but still legible: *Eve Cavell, 71700.*

Rationing breath, she marks the number.

All night she has rehearsed, repeating to herself again and again the words she will say to Eve, and imagining what Eve will say in return. She imagines Eve's voice, breathy and childlike, the voice of a woman who lives alone and recites poetry to the stray dogs that pass beneath her window. She imagines Eve's soft manicured hands lifting up the receiver, the lonely look on her face, the yearning in her eyes. She imagines Eve not so very different from herself.

"Hello?" she hears a woman say in an accent she has heard on Voice of America.

"Alo."

She strains to remember the words for all that she's feeling and wishing and wanting to make right, but none occur to her. She'd like to tell Eve about reading the forbidden books, about all the tangled daydreams that distract her while she's rearranging the clutter in her brother's room.

"Salim must marry you," she emits with conviction. "It is correct."

"Who are you?" the voice asks.

Amal pictures Eve opening the curtain and gazing out over the rooftops to the window where she huddles groping for words. She imagines Eve near, beside her, reaching out from the darkness with the perfect baby boy cradled in her arms.

"I am...your sister," Amal says and, satisfied, replaces the receiver.

AT THE ALLENBY BRIDGE

Salim Mahmoud steps out into the ominous stillness of a Jerusalem night, a little drunk, but not drunk enough to feel safe, or happy, or to believe in a God that cares whether he wins the lottery or dies.

He has stayed out past curfew, dragging himself like unclaimed baggage from the bed of his sleeping lover. He will not dream tonight. Not with the sirens wailing and his wristwatch alarm set for seven a.m.

He pictures Eve as he left her, limbs and breasts and dark ringlets strewn like treasure atop the common white sheets. Asleep, thighs parted. Asleep, trusting. He had draped a shawl across her nakedness, turned off the lights, locked the door. He had done what any decent man would do.

As he drops dead weight into the driver's seat of his Datsun, he has the urge to glance up at her balcony. She has awakened, come out to watch him go. She doesn't wave a hand in farewell, only stands in the darkness, staring after him like a sea wife. He wishes he were drunk enough to crawl back to her bed and stay there until the world ends. He hesitates, muttering curses in French and Arabic onto the steering wheel, and drunk—but not drunk enough—turns the key in the ignition.

Salim tosses three sugar cubes into a cup of grainy black coffee and downs it hurriedly, scalding his tongue. He has a hangover, but only a small one, and no reason to think that today will be any better or any worse than yesterday.

Car keys in hand, he steps into the foyer. Confronting the full-length mirror beside the front door, he inspects himself with the critical eye of a man who aspires to perfection. The crease in his pants hangs straight as a plumb-line. His seasoned Bally brogues, recently resoled, shine like shwarma on a spit. He runs a comb through his hair, which to his chagrin has begun to recede, and makes a mental note to pass by Jaffa Road after work and shop for a hat.

He has a few shekels in his wallet—not enough to see him through until payday but more than some weeks—and his friend Costa has offered to float him a loan until he can ask his tightwad Jewish boss for a raise.

From a distance he hears his mother call, "Salim, rushing off again? A letter's come, from your cousin Sameeha..." High heels clacking overhead like hammer blows.

He looks into the mirror, into his own eyes, red-rimmed from too much alcohol and too little sleep, and feels the urge to run. Yanking open the oversized mahogany door, he crosses the threshold to a deceptive freedom, the street quiet and the air almost clear. He's late for work, but not as late as usual. His Datsun starts on the third try. Exhaling relief, he revs the engine and drives the four blocks to Jaffa Gate.

As he parks the car and steps into the helter-skelter traffic skirting the Old City, he wonders for a moment what became of the oddly dressed street preacher who once haunted the gate and tries to remember what it was the man used to say. Something about God's arm, he vaguely recalls, and the hard time sinners can expect on the Day of Judgment. Christian theatrics, intended no doubt to bring shame on unrepentant heathen like himself. But Salim, having lived on the fault line between doom and salvation for as long as he remembers, can only think about today.

Today he will sell baubles behind the jewelry counter of Sterns, he will buy a hat, change the car oil...the things any sane person might do to stay alive. *Inshallah*, may the big boss upstairs so dispose, he will be spared the arbitrary bullet or knife thrust, and survive to bury himself in his lover's body one more time. One more time.

Pulses slow, glasses fill, and a low din of conversation competes with the tinny hum of music played on an antiquated sound system. Salim raises a snifter of Rémy Martin to eye level, its amber glow a beacon in the perpetual twilight of the American Colony Hotel. Seated at a plate-sized table in the jazz cellar, a place at once familiar and foreign with its cadre of international journalists and diplomats, its smattering of influential Palestinians, he can almost feel pleased with himself. Here, his surname still counts for something. The bartender remembers his drink and the waiters stand at attention, waiting to flick a lighter each time he reaches for his box of Rothmans.

"Cheers, *habibi*," he says, dear fellow, toasting his friend Costa, the two young men loosening their ties, lighting up.

Costa cocks his shot glass.

"To our good fortune." He eyes a trio of fair-haired women seated across the lounge. "The redhead's mine—not that the blonde's bad either. Germans, I'll wager."

Salim surveys the room and finds a woman more to his liking on the opposite side, younger, with a small but conspicuous tattoo adorning her nubile shoulder.

"Take all three."

The young men sit back and blow smoke rings, Salim tapping time on the tabletop to a fifties rendition of "Satin Doll," Costa casting lovesick glances at the chosen redhead.

"They've gotten so political, the tourists," he laments. "Time was you bought a woman a few drinks, impressed her with your knowledge of art or French, and she'd invite you back to her hotel room. Now they all want to talk about the Two-State Solution. They want to go back home and be able to tell their friends that they made love with a freedom fighter."

"If that's what it takes, I'll be Arafat." Salim puffs out his chest. "I'll be Abu Nidal."

Salim grew up in a household rent by political clashes, with no ideology of his own. A skeptic by nature, hedonist by choice, he sees nothing to be gained by hoisting flags or chanting slogans. Secretly, he admires the Americans, whose constitutionally guaranteed pursuit of happiness he considers a stroke of genius.

Costa makes an ideal companion. The pair, schoolmates since prepuberty, share the same skepticism of Palestinian nationalism, the same hankering for foreign women of dubious morals. Not only are their vices complementary, but their combined assets give them a strategic advantage. Whereas Salim has his good looks and family connections to fall back on, Costa has ready cash. He can always be counted on to bankroll a critical round of drinks.

Costa's redhead stands up and saunters toward the exit, followed in tight formation by her companions. Costa's shoulders slump.

Signaling the waiter for another whiskey, he says glumly, "The situation's not good, *habibi*."

"When has it ever been?"

"My father's restaurant is going under. The leaflets tell him to close, the soldiers tell him to open. Open, close, open...it's giving the old guy the shakes."

"If a thing isn't white, it's black."

"No, my friend," Costa says, muffling his voice with an unsteady hand, "it's all turned gray. Who to believe? Who to trust?"

# # #

Sometimes Salim wonders what his life would be like if the borders had shifted west instead of east. Other Mahmouds, second and third cousins whose property remained on the Jordanian side of the divide after the War of '67, have fared better. They have money.

It irks Salim to be a poor relative. It irks him to have his mother forever plotting propitious marriages to distant cousins no one else wants, old maids, whom Salim barely knows and whose conspicuous virginity he finds depressing.

On his rare visits to Jordan—he's been turned back at the Allenby Bridge as often as allowed across—the chic appearance and lordly demeanor of his mother's family make him feel shabby, a beggar. They speak of their vacations in the south of France, their soirees in the homes of Hashemite royalty, their latest purchase of talking computers or limited-edition lithographs, and he has no choice but to pay court, complimenting them—sometimes sincerely, more often not—on their good taste. They are generous, proper Muslims, as Salim himself might be in their place. He can't hate them. It isn't their fault they have what he can only dream of. His anger and his wanting aren't their fault.

So much easier to blame the Zionists, who by brute force and deception have dispossessed the Mahmouds of everything but their innate nobility. Gone, the palaces. Gone, the olive groves. Gone, the privilege and the power that kept his ancestors at the center of Jerusalem society through countless changes of regime.

Each time Salim crosses paths with a soldier, he relives the war. He remembers those six endless days as clearly as his last meal or the first time he entered a woman. He had been adding stamps to his album when the fighting erupted. He and his mother, then pregnant with his only sister, took refuge in the basement storeroom of the King George Hotel. It was a wretched place, damp, dark, but well provisioned. An elderly uncle kept an eye on them. He had brought along a transistor radio and held it clasped to an ear day and night.

"The Arab forces are victorious on all fronts," he would report in an excited whisper. "The Jews are fleeing...West Jerusalem's a ruin...the Egyptian army is taking tea in the Knesset."

On the seventh day an unshaven contingent of Israeli soldiers threw open the doors of the storeroom and led them out into a chaos of reversed fortunes. The Jews were everywhere, dancing like fools in their circular hats, racing in droves toward the Western Wall. Salim and his mother walked home in silence.

As they neared the house, he heard her utter, "There is nothing left for us," and begin to sob.

Salim ran ahead, bewildered and calling as loudly as he dared for his pet Persian cat, Soleil. It didn't take him long to find the cat; he knew all of her favorite haunts. On the roof she was, lying with paws outstretched on a sunny spot beside the parapet.

Salim had entered the house, scavenged the icebox, and climbed the spiral staircase to his bedroom. Opening the window, he extended a saucer of sour milk toward the cat, the only thing he had to offer her.

"Drink, kitty," he cooed, and waited for her to slink across the tiles and submerge her whiskers.

But Soleil didn't move. Front paws pointing east, rear stretching west, she lay inert in the sunlight, shot precisely in half by a shell. *Precisely*, Salim would later tell his friends, as if the Jews had measured the poor creature from end to end before inflicting the death blow.

Salim turns the key in the lock and slowly opens the front door, which squeaks more loudly than he'd like it to, considering the hour.

The bar closed at midnight. Eve had been sleeping when he

entered her flat and drew the sheets down about her ankles. He hadn't stayed long. But his Datsun stalled across the street from Damascus Gate, and he'd left it there, nervously walking the last few blocks home. A jeep-load of soldiers had stopped him on Salah-ah-Din Street and asked to see his identity card.

He arrived home in a dark mood, despite the alcohol coursing through his bloodstream and the sense memory of Eve's body opening to him like a late-blooming orchid.

In the foyer he pauses, waits for his eyes to adjust to the darkness. He unties and removes his shoes. Without switching on a light, he begins to ascend the staircase, stumbling up the steps two at a time. As he nears the top a door opens, revealing the angular silhouette of his sister, Amal.

"Brother," she whispers, "I've been waiting for you."

With a timid gesture, she motions him into her bedroom and soundlessly closes the door.

One small lamp illumines the room, which is spacious and furnished with an unmatched array of old furniture, much like his own. His sister wears a gray flannel robe, white anklets, and round-toed flats the color of porridge. Her appearance, not only her clothes but the self-effacing way she wears them, embarrasses him. To Salim, her plainness suggests mutant genes. He has heard relatives refer to her as a molting bird.

"Up so late?" He reaches into his shirt pocket for a breath mint. He doesn't take a seat. "Bloody soldiers hassled me again," he mutters.

Amal folds her hands and begins to pace.

"Something has happened. Mother had wanted to tell you, but her nerves—you know how she is. Aunt Sana finally got her to take a sedative."

Salim, abruptly sober, takes his sister by the arm.

"Our mother overreacts. Every headline unsettles her nerves."

Amal, eyes lowered, whispers, "It's Costa. He's…they say, he's…dead."

"Nonsense," Salim snaps. "I saw him, couldn't have been more than a few hours ago."

Amal begins to cry.

"They found his body on the road to Gaza."

"An accident?"

With a vehemence that stuns Salim, she clutches him by both shoulders and rasps, "There are no accidents anymore. They say he was a collaborator. They say the strike forces killed him. The Israelis found him in a ditch with his tongue cut out."

Salim reels toward the door and drives a fist into the varnished mahogany.

"Lies!"

He can feel Amal come up behind him and place a small, almost weightless, hand on his arm.

"Lies they may be, but we're all sick with fright. If they killed Costa—whoever killed Costa—don't you see, Salim? You can't stay in Jerusalem."

Cradling his throbbing fist, he crosses the corridor to his room and collapses onto the bed without undressing. His prone body twitches. Bolting upright, he switches on the chandelier. For a long time he stands in the middle of the room and stares at a moth, the flimsy creature hurling itself against the lit bulbs and dropping to the floor with broken wings.

Eve greets him at the door, smiling her sad half-smile, a yellow crocus pinned in her black hair.

"You're early tonight," she says, a question.

Salim takes her by the waist. "I couldn't wait to see you."

A leather journal lies open on the kitchen table. In passing, he turns a few pages.

"Writing?"

"I haven't written in weeks. Who has words anymore? The broken bones, the knifings, people burning trees..."

He places a finger at the juncture of her lips. "Hush."

"And pretend not to see?"

"We agreed not to talk about it."

They lean into each other, his chin grazes the crown of her head. They retain this posture for a moment, neither speaking. Salim's chest warms where Eve's breath meets it. Her nearness makes him think of lace and lightning, of the color red, the taste of ripe persimmons. Deaf to his own sighs, blind to everything but her skin, he leads her from the kitchen to the bedroom and plucks the flower from her hair.

"I'll put on music," she murmurs.

"Ravel."

Watching her cross the room, he changes his mind and summons her back.

Whether or not he loves her, he'll never know. He only knows this urgency, the need to sacrifice himself to the flashfire of her hips. She is his *houri*, the beautiful woman he'll never see in paradise. Lips sweeter than the wells of Jericho, thighs like the two Niles parting...and the night so long.

He leaves her asleep, pausing at the bedstead to watch her breasts peek through the weave of a thin white shawl. A full moon hangs framed in the window. Navigating by its waning light, he feels beneath the edge of the coverlet for his shoes and socks, puts them on, locks the door, and descends the narrow staircase to the wind-whipped street. He sprints the few steps to his car and drops into the driver's seat.

Gazing mechanically over the steering wheel, he watches Eve glide onto the balcony, naked except for the shawl and searching for his eyes. She has placed a blues collection on the CD player, ballads as torpid and bittersweet as the sound of a heart breaking.

"Go back inside," he shouts.

As he pulls away, he can feel her eyes follow him. He feels her in his cells. She's in his breath. Jerking the gearshift into reverse, he races backward and slams on the brakes. He gets out of the car, and falling to his knees in the glare of the headlights, cries, "It's impossible, face it! Let me be."

Salim crosses the Allenby Bridge, feet swelling in stiff new shoes, back clammy with sweat.

On the Jordanian side, coolly appraising in a chauffeur-driven Mercedes sedan, sit Salim's cousin Sameeha and her mother. As he approaches, the driver emerges and steps grudgingly forward to take his generic vinyl suitcase. Salim extracts a silk handkerchief from the breast pocket of his blazer and fans himself with it, hoping his relatives will notice the Pierre Cardin logo along its edge.

"*Salaam aleicham*," the matriarch greets him, extending a gloved hand through the half-open car window. Then, in excruciatingly correct French, "Welcome, nephew."

Salim glances past her to his cousin Sameeha, who, seated with legs crossed at the ankle, averts her eyes.

"You're keeping well, cousin," he says, inclining in her direction and noticing with concealed distaste her planed chest and thin colorless lips.

Sameeha only nods at him. Her mother responds for her, "We've just returned from the most marvelous new spa. The kilos simply melt away."

The driver slowly circles the car and opens the front passenger seat door. Salim hesitates. Looking back toward the bridge, he feels his life shrink to the size of a fist. The future has been arranged for him: he will work for a rich uncle, marry Sameeha, inseminate her. Their children will grow up Muslims in a Muslim country. What sane person wouldn't be grateful, he tells himself.

"Get in, nephew," Sameeha's mother says with thinly veiled impatience. "I don't like the smell here."

Salim seats himself beside the driver. He would like to remove his sport jacket but is afraid his relatives will see the perspiration stains rimming his armpits. He would like to loosen his tie.

In the rearview mirror he catches sight of Sameeha, her homely face quietly triumphant.

He feels not the least desire for her, but he vows to himself—at the first opportunity—to rip her overpriced silk dress to ribbons and cover her puny breasts with love bites. He hates her for being proud and untouchable. He hates the studied way she acknowledges his gaze, as if proffering a gift he can never repay.

A MOTHER OF SOLDIERS

Leah Halevi awakens with a shudder, the nightmare a shadow on her pillow, her bed empty. There was a time—not long ago, she reminds herself—when her husband, Jacob, would stir beside her, reach out a hand, and ask, "That same dream?"

She would nod.

Again, her husband's sleepy voice: "Which one was it this time, Amnon or Dov?"

Every night for all her life as a mother Leah has suffered the death of one or the other of her sons. She watches, helpless, as a masked sniper riddles her elder boy's muscular body with bullets. She sees the younger kidnapped by terrorists and left in a dumpster to suffocate. Sometimes she sees them blown to pieces by a suicide bomber, both of them simultaneously—but this she never told her husband. There are limits to how much misery a sentient being can absorb. Perhaps Jacob had reached his by then.

Jacob had always been a little different from other people, more sensitive. She'd known him since childhood, the scrawny blue-eyed orphan unloaded by the Jewish Agency on Kibbutz Sde Boker after World War II, the doted-upon adolescent whom Ben-Gurion treated like his own son, the brilliant engineering student upon whom the kibbutz elders pinned their hopes for the future. His metamorphosis had been hers also. She grew into a woman worthy of him, a degreed psychologist in private practice, devoted mother, faithful wife. They made a good couple, she persists in believing. For twenty-nine years they never once failed to make love on the Sabbath.

His leaving has shaken all illusion from her life. No longer can she believe that vows cement hearts together or that decades of laundering and neatly folding a man's jockey shorts entitle her to a modicum of security. One moment Jacob had been repairing the caulking along the bathtub, the next tearing shirts from their hangers and stuffing them into a duffel bag.

"Reserve duty again?" she had asked, distracted by the hiss of a pot of beef barley soup boiling over on the stove.

He had frozen in place.

"I can't stay here. It's not fair to you."

She didn't need to ask what he meant. Her husband had always been transparent to her, like the see-through anatomical dummies they'd used at university to teach her about reproduction and pathology. She knew he was in love with another woman. She felt it each time he pushed his plate away half-full or sat staring into the distance with an open book on his lap.

"Nothing has happened between her and me, you understand," he hastened to add, "but I…have thoughts."

"What about our sons?" she said with what remained of her voice.

Jacob hunched over his duffel bag then and his shoulders began to quiver. His muffled sobs sounded to Leah like doves cooing on a desert night. She remembered Sde Boker and the evenings she and Jacob had spent strolling through the long rows of date palms, their dreams stretched out before them like a bounty waiting to be claimed.

That she would one day find herself abandoned, a crone haunted in her own bed—unthinkable, a mistake. She had chosen wisely. She had loved well. Every morning for twenty-nine years she had risen at daybreak to bring her husband a cup of tea with a sprig of fresh mint.

An Arab woman and her young son would come to the apartment door once a week, selling the mint, strings of Bedouin figs, pomegranates, sesame paste, and bitter lemons. Leah had watched the boy grow from a sticky-mouthed toddler into a brooding adolescent. One night, as he handed her change from a five-shekel note, their gazes locked and Leah read in his eyes, one day I will kill your sons. From then on those eyes became the focal point of her nightmare, swearing with every glance to destroy what her love for Jacob had created.

Leah rouses and pushes back the sheets. She swings her legs over the side of the bed, slips into two pink puffs of slipper, and pads to the bathroom. As she splashes icy water onto her cheeks, the mirror above the basin casts back the image of someone who might once have been pretty. She looks away. Whatever gravity spares, time will take, but she needn't be a witness.

Returning to her bedroom, she pulls on a pair of faded Levi's and a Hebrew University sweatshirt, then replaces the enormous cotton candy-like slippers. Her hair she tugs back and secures at the nape with a rubber band. Although it's Saturday and she has no appointments to keep, she reaches mechanically for her Seiko wristwatch, a gift from Jacob on their silver wedding anniversary.

Amnon and Dov have come home for the Sabbath, hitchhiking from army bases at opposite ends of the country. They will sleep late. By breakfast they'll be ravenous. Grateful for a task, she puts the kettle on and takes out a mixing bowl.

For a moment the familiarity of the motions, the solid feel of the utensils, returns her to the before time. Humming to herself, she gazes toward the kitchen table, half expecting to find her family there; Jacob skimming the morning's headlines, the two boys dunking cinnamon toast into chocolate milk. But all she sees are her sons' matching rifles, slung across a chairback.

Leah can pinpoint the exact moment when her husband fell in love with the other woman.

It was a *Shabbat* afternoon in early spring. She had invited Mozes Koenig, an old friend of the family, for the traditional meal of cholent. Mozes, something of a hermit in recent years, had brought along the heroine of his latest novel, an unfocused-looking young American he introduced as Eve.

Leah, busy arranging food on platters and carrying it to the dining room table, hadn't paid much attention to her at first.

"Get Mozes some Tokaji," she had called across the room to Amnon, "and bring an extra chair."

Jacob arrived from work moments later, carrying a box of the hand-dipped chocolates that were her one indulgence. Only Dov was absent, posted too far away to make the trip home. From the kitchen she could hear glasses clinking and snippets of conversation. Jacob chiding Mozes, "Where have you been hiding?" and Mozes retorting, "I fell through a trap door."

Leah placed bowls heaped with hummous and stuffed green olives on the already cluttered table. In passing she noticed the purple ribbon in Eve's hair and heard her make some cryptic remark about the golden age of American jazz. Not until the main course had been dished out, however, did she pause long enough to assess her rival's finely sculpted face and torso and the way Jacob's eyes lingered on her mouth, which was full-lipped and painted the color of fire.

"The black iris," he was saying, "a rare blossom with a beauty all its own. I'll take you to see it, if you like."

Leah didn't remind Jacob that he had once compared her to that same flower, a betrayal she would later confide to her diary. Dissembling her wounded pride behind a sham serenity, she had removed the soiled dinner plates. An old 45 droned on the turntable—Barber's *Medea*, it may have been. The teapot whistled. Mozes and Eve began chattering about some obscure Sufi poet she had never heard of. "Mystical, ecstatic, transcendent!" Mozes brandished his wine glass. "Kabir made a religion of poetry."

"No, not a religion," Eve protested in a deceptively mild voice. With seeming innocence she drew the ribbon from her hair and let the plaits flow onto her shoulders. Then, in a stage whisper, "Kabir gave voice to the soul itself."

Jacob, shunting aside the rice pudding Leah had placed before him, all but groaned, "I must hear it."

Twice stung, Leah blurted, "Patent nonsense. If the soul could speak, no doubt it would tell us to stop all this navel-gazing."

Jacob slumped forward onto his elbows and looked directly at Eve.

"I'd like to believe there is such a thing, a soul."

The room filled with shadows, with blinding stabs of truth. Leah took stock: twenty-nine years of marriage and her husband behaving like a naive adolescent. The pudding untouched. It did not bode well.

Then Eve closed her eyes and recited, *"Make your supple body sing, let it be the sunlit infinite song of flowers,"* and Leah knew she had lost him. It had barely taken a moment, a line of gibberish, to undo her life.

Amnon shuffles into the kitchen, unshaven and rubbing the sleep from his eyes.

"*Boker tov,*" he murmurs, good morning.

He is wearing a flannel pajama top that once belonged to Jacob and a pair of sweatpants. His thick black hair, tousled, emanates a faint scent of wood smoke. He has his father's blue eyes, his square jaw, the same soft-spoken way about him.

"There's waffles," Leah says, already preparing his plate. "Dov still sleeping?"

Amnon nods, pours himself a cup of tea.

Leah, lowering her voice, ventures, "I don't like the way your brother's been behaving. Always tired, and so quiet."

"The army's hard on you at first, night duty and all that. He'll get used to it."

"I know my own son," she insists. "It's not like Dov to bottle up this way. Something's wrong."

"You worry too much."

She reaches for Friday's *Ha'Aretz* and skims the headlines.

"Another kidnapped soldier...Syria's up to more monkey business in Lebanon...and that megalomaniacal Iraqi is threatening to invade Kuwait. How not to worry?" She takes a squeeze bottle of maple syrup from the cupboard and places it on the lazy susan. "Have you read about that new game kids have invented?" she goes on, gesturing toward the street with a slotted spoon. "Throwing themselves in front of moving cars—is this the behavior of normal children? We're raising a generation of kamikazes."

Amnon shrugs his shoulders and continues to eat. Leah, collecting herself, refills his teacup.

"Have you kept in touch with your father?"

"He calls."

"Have you seen him?"

"We had coffee."

"How does he look?"

"Fine."

She paces in front of the kitchen window, catching glimpses of people walking dogs and getting into parked cars. An Orthodox woman pushes a baby stroller. The new neighbor—some sort of artist, judging by the paint stains on his hands—jogs along the lane, adjusting the Sony Walkman wired to his head. Yemin Moshe has changed in recent years, gentrified. Leah misses the old Slavic women who used to gather on doorsteps with their embroidery hoops, she misses the ice seller, misses even the peeling paint.

"Your father and I used to picnic across the street in the park. There were more songbirds then. The air was cleaner."

Amnon pushes his chair back from the table and stretches out his legs.

"Maybe you should take a vacation."

Leah forces a laugh.

"Where would I go? Club Med?"

She switches on the radio, flicks the dial, turns it off again.

"You think I'm losing my marbles, don't you?"

Amnon veers his gaze toward the doorway, where younger brother Dov stands shifting his weight from one slippered foot to the other. Leah nods in his direction and, reaching numbly for the teapot, dries a stray tear on the sleeve of her sweatshirt.

"A vacation...I'll think about it," she says.

With her eyes casting about in bare-lidded vigilance, Leah dashes through Jaffa Gate at a breathless clip and veers right. Since the yeshiva student got knifed on his way home from the Western Wall, she has avoided the Old City. "Better to wait it out," Jacob would say. But at forty-nine, Leah—never a patient woman—is tired of waiting.

Just beyond the half-resurrected Cardo Maximus with its scaffolds and its T-shirt shops, she turns into a narrow lane, approaches a cracked unswept doorstep, and craning her neck calls out, "Mozes, I know you're in there."

The old hermit has stopped returning her phone calls since Jacob left home.

"Don't worry, I'm not going to bite your head off."

She hears footsteps, a hand on the door latch, her friend's voice saying, "Promise?"

Mozes opens the door and, stepping to one side, motions her up a staircase and into the dingy parlor of his flat. He's wearing a faded silk bathrobe and holding a worn leather eyeshade.

"Pardon the mayhem." He takes a stack of newspapers from the armchair and tosses them onto a coffee table. "Sit, *boubala*, I'll bring you a nice cup of something."

Facing him with hands on hips, Leah snarls, "Spare me the tea and sympathy routine. Just tell me what your Jezebel's up to with my husband."

Mozes draws into himself.

"Are they lovers?" Leah prods him.

"Who can account for the human heart?"

"That's no answer. Anyone with eyes can tell when two people are in love."

He pouts. "You blame me."

"No one's to blame." Momentarily spent, she collapses into the armchair and curls forward, chin in hand. "You marry, you think you know someone, you dream on the same pillow…Oh shit, Mozes, I'm starting to sound like one of those bleeding hearts on the soap operas."

She takes a book from her tote bag and holds it aloft.

"Your latest."

Mozes' face reddens. He fidgets with the sash of his bathrobe. "Then, you've read it?"

"Of course, I've read it. I'm your biggest fan—or have you forgotten? You signed my copy of A *Time for War* nearly ten years ago. I gave it to my sons before they started army duty. I told them, there comes a time when you've got to choose your corner and defend the things you love. Exactly what Hannah told Shlomo in chapter six.

Every mother in Israel has shed tears over that scene." She places the book on the chair arm, leaving her empty hands to gesture with recharged vigor. "And now, decades later, comes the long-awaited sequel. A *Time for Peace*, you have the chutzpah to call it. Now you tell us, throw your guns into the Jordan River and make love. Now, instead of heroes, you give us an American slut and her Arab Don Juan. *This* is literature?"

Mozes rises and walks to the window.

"Whatever possessed you," she rails at his retreating back, "to write about a woman who has nothing better to do than sleep with Arabs and ponder her Jewish identity? Jewish indeed—didn't you say her father was a gentile?"

"*Nu?*"

"This Eve. This half-breed nobody who's not worth Hannah's little finger, if you ask me. What Jacob sees in her, I can't imagine. But then, you're probably head over heels with her yourself."

"Have you read the poems of Radnoti?" He looks out above the ramparts. "The last ones were recovered from his corpse, exhumed from a mass grave after the War. He wrote them in a concentration camp. Love poems...imagine."

She crosses the room and gazes over his shoulder through the sooty windowpane.

"What a fine pair of fools we are, Mozes."

He turns and shrugs his bearish shoulders. "Who's trying to win a popularity contest?"

He opens his arms to her, familiar old arms that remind her of wheat sheaves and yesterdays.

"Will Jacob come back?"

"If only I knew, *boubala*..."

Leah tastes the vegetable soup simmering on the stove, adds salt. She gets down her dog-eared Betty Crocker cookbook, a wedding gift from her mother, and turns to the section called Potatoes, Rice, Legumes. Cooking without appetite demands all the concentration she can muster. Forcing herself to focus on the yellowed pages, she reads aloud, "Simple yet elegant…can be prepared ahead of time…garnish with chopped parsley."

A faded birth announcement marks the page with Jacob's favorite, Rice Pilaf with Almonds and Mushrooms. "For a taste of the exotic…" She'd have to go to the Arab market for saffron. No chance of that. And besides, the boys would be just as happy with french-fried potatoes. She closes the cookbook, opens the cupboard. And suddenly, she'd like to lie down, draw the curtains, pull a blanket over her head.

Depression, she diagnoses.

The front door squeaks open.

"Dov?" she calls.

"No, *ima*. It's Amnon."

She had expected her younger son, posted in recent weeks within minutes of Jerusalem, to arrive first.

"You're home early." She walks into the living room with a bottle of safflower oil in one hand and a paring knife in the other. Rising onto her toes, she angles her cheek toward him for a kiss. "I picked up some books at Steimatsky's—that college guide you asked for and the latest Oz. They're on your bed."

Amnon lowers his duffel onto the carpet.

"Laundry?"

He nods and takes the rifle from his shoulder.

"Let's sit down for a minute, huh?" he says, beginning to lead her toward the sofa.

"After I get these potatoes frying. You know your brother, always arrives bottomless like some starving Ethiopian."

Amnon removes the knife from her hand and nudges her gently into the nearest chair.

"That can wait. Dov won't be coming home today."

Leah clutches her bottle of oil and utters, "No?"

"He's all right," Amnon hastens to say, "but he might not be home…for a while."

"Lebanon?"

"Prison."

A nervous laugh spills over Leah's lips.

"If I didn't know better…you can't mean…"

"He's been court-martialed for refusing to serve in the territories. Twenty-one days, they gave him."

Leah bolts to her feet and makes for the telephone.

"Your father will take care of this," she says crisply. "If Dov's commander is being difficult, we'll just have to go over his head. Some bigwig's bound to owe Jacob a favor." She glances at her wristwatch. "Knowing him, he'll still be at the office."

"I've already tried calling," Amnon murmurs.

Her hand wavers on the receiver.

"It's no use, *ima*. He's out of the country attending a conference. His secretary says he's not expected back for another ten days."

Leah hears the breath drain out of her as if from a punctured tire. She thinks, if Jacob hadn't left, this would never have happened. Dov would be home. Her family would be gathered at the table, sipping sweet Sabbath wine and sharing the week's news.

"How long have you known?" she asks tonelessly.

"I didn't think he'd go through with it." Her son sinks deeper into the sofa with his bullish shoulders sloping. "Lots of guys talk about it. I mean, who *wants* to face off with a bunch of angry kids in some refugee camp?" He pauses, avoiding her eyes. Then, with the timbre of his voice grown sharp, "Dov's commander was a sonuvabitch Arab-hater. Dov knew what could happen under a commander like that once you cross the Green Line. So, he drew his own line."

The sun-blistered asphalt highway bubbles like molten lava. Leah floors the accelerator, eyes flitting from the rearview mirror to the roadsides to the oncoming traffic.

Beside her, Mozes Koenig, mottle-faced from motion sickness, rasps, "Practicing for the Grand Prix?"

"Roll up that window," she orders. "Don't you listen to the news? Innocent people burned alive in buses—it's not just stones these kids are throwing anymore."

They pass the Mount of Olives and turn east, toward Jericho. Midway between the two ancient cities, cut into bare cliff, is a place called Wadi Qilt, where her son Dov serves time in a makeshift prison.

"Elijah the Prophet hid in a cave near there," muses Mozes. "A troubler of Israel, that's what Ahab called him." In a surfeit of zeal he brings his fist down on the dashboard. "Don't you see the parallel?"

"My son's no prophet," Leah replies with undisguised irritation. "Stubborn, that's what he is. Even as a kid he was always getting into debates for refusing to call Judea and Samaria by their biblical names. The *occupied territories*, he insisted on saying."

"He took a stand."

"Let someone else give the generals indigestion. My son's got a future to think about. This is Israel, not New Zealand. Life's hard enough without getting on the wrong side of the Israeli Defense Forces." She swerves to avoid hitting a run-over cat. "Light me a cigarette, will you?"

Mozes says meekly, "I thought you didn't smoke."

"I don't."

They drive the rest of the way in silence.

The landscape alternates between gray and gray-yellow; glare blurs all but the harshest edges. With the windows closed, a staleness pervades the atmosphere. Leah tugs open her collar. Slow-moving trucks spew diesel fumes onto the windshield.

As the sun peaks, a squat concrete building flanked by a towering metal pole comes into view. The Israeli flag with its blue Star of David hangs lank in the stagnant air.

"This must be it." Leah skids off the asphalt onto a bulldozed swath of tired earth and brings the car to an abrupt halt. She yanks open the door and leaps out with a cardboard carton clasped to her bosom and her tote bag thudding against her ribs. "Aren't you coming?" she calls to Mozes.

"You go ahead."

She steers a crooked course through the parked jeeps and dumpsters. Beside the entrance a girl soldier extends a hand toward her bulging satchel.

"I've brought some things for my son."

The girl, expressionless and well-trained, conducts a routine search.

"And the box?"

"Books," Leah answers, beginning to stoop under the load.

"Leave them there."

The girl points toward a card table with a cracked vinyl top. Beneath it, a coiled cat naps in the scant shade.

"I'll put Dov's name on the flap," Leah thinks aloud, already taking the Cross pen from the breast pocket of her blouse.

Willing her hand steady and her head erect, she writes in large block letters. Her son might be a prisoner of the state, but she needn't cower before his jailers. Soundless in rubber-soled combat boots, the soldier comes up beside her.

"Are you Dov's mother?" she asks, dropping any pretense of formality.

Leah nods.

"Don't worry, we're looking out for him."

"We?"

"Those of us on the Left," she says with a conspiratorial wink. "Look, he could have wound up in Prison Six. This joint's the Hotel Dan in comparison." Escorting Leah through the door, she calls to a uniformed clerk, "Halevi on break?"

The clerk waves Leah toward a folding chair, vanishes through a swinging door, and reappears moments later with her son.

Dov wears an army uniform, for which she's grateful. Nothing marks him as a prisoner—nothing but the fact that he carries no gun.

"*Ima*," he whispers tentatively, leaning down to kiss her cheek.

"You could have told me."

A door at the rear of the room opens, and through it Leah glimpses a handcuffed Arab kneeling in the courtyard with a burlap sack covering his head and neck. She sees this with her own eyes yet every rational fiber of her says, *a lie*. Such things don't happen in a civilized country.

"You had enough to deal with," her son replies, taking a seat beside her. He crosses and uncrosses his arms. "There are things a person has to do alone. I don't expect you to be proud of me."

Leah continues to stare at the now closed door.

"My parents helped build this country," she says absently. "By sunrise they were in the fields breaking their backs. All those years of sacrifice…for what? For what?"

Dov leans forward with fists dug into his temples. The soles of his boots grind into the linoleum.

"I don't know. It's going wrong somehow."

"We had such dreams…"

"Things can't get better until we stop pretending we're the only people here, the only ones who matter."

"It's not a question of who matters," she counters wearily, her voice hollow, the conviction wrung from it. "When you put on that uniform, you agreed to protect your people."

"There are limits. Does protecting my people mean breaking bones, axing olive trees, blowing up a family's home? I can't. I won't."

Leah clasps her son's hand.

"What happens now?"

"They could try to send me back," he says, "in which case I would refuse again."

"And be sentenced again?"

Dov shrugs.

"We're too much alike," Leah says, shrugging in turn. "Hard-headed." She sits studying her son, remembering the talkative trusting boy he had once been, and the words she'd been trying not to say escape in a surge of impotent rage: "There's no going back—and even if there were, the one thing I can't give you is a life of easy choices."

The odor of chlorine and fried falafel shrouds the salty lick of sea air. The lapping of the waves gets lost in a relentless din of loudspeaker rock-and-roll.

Leah squeezes a shekel-sized puddle of tanning lotion into the palm of her hand and spreads it on her thighs. The years have taken the bloom from her skin. She surveys the damage through dark glasses, her wasteland of a body gone to seed within an out-of-fashion bathing suit purchased before the birth of her sons.

At Amnon's urging, she has come south to the seaside resort of

Eilat for a few days' rest. All around her, greased bodies in varying states of disrepair sprawl on lounge chairs, huddle beneath beach umbrellas, splash in the kidney-shaped pool. She supposes they're having fun. She supposes this is how people cope with the pressures of holding together a life.

Maneuvering onto her stomach she stares in the direction of the poolside bar, a thatched structure encircled by rattan chairs. Her polarized lenses collide with the squinting eyes of a man in jungle-print bathing trunks. He grins at her. She fumbles beneath the chair for her weathered copy of *The Wisdom of Insecurity* and peers at him over her eyeglass frames. There's something vaguely familiar about him, which troubles her. She wouldn't want to be seen like this—alone, idle, her bare limbs slick as basting chicken parts—by anyone she knows. Unable to place the stranger, she brings the paperback to eye level and pretends to read.

"Funny us running into each other so far from home," she hears someone say in Anglicized Hebrew.

The man in the jungle-print trunks has stretched out on the next lounge chair with a tropical drink in his hand and a beach towel draped across his sunburnt belly.

Having never had the patience for small talk, Leah doesn't respond immediately. The forced leisure has begun to cloy. She sits up, pulls on an oversized T-shirt, and is about to excuse herself when she notices the man's paint-stained hands.

"I'm an artist," he says in explanation. "My studio's in Yemin Moshe. I've seen you there."

"Small country." She slips quickly into her rubber beach shoes.

"You're Leah Halevi, aren't you? I heard you once on a talk show. I liked what you had to say about the effects of violence on youth."

She sits back down.

"Do you have children?"

"A girl, back in England. She lives with my ex-wife."

Leah stares into the distance, letting the sea breeze caress her face and trying to remember when she and Jacob last visited Hyde Park.

"You must let me buy you a drink," the man says, motioning for a waiter. "They make a walloping frozen daiquiri here."

Leah is about to say, I don't drink.

"A few of these and you won't have a care in the world."

Allowing herself a whim, she acquiesces, removes the paper umbrella from the rim of the tumbler, and applies her chapped lips to the drinking straw.

Her companion proposes a toast: "To you. To chance meetings. To the great mystery of love."

Leah, having never flirted before, has no handy cache of stock responses. Conscious that she's behaving out of character, daring herself to, she accepts a cigarette and drains her glass. For ten whole minutes she doesn't think about her family.

"Are you trying to seduce me?" she muses.

"Are you suggesting I seduce you?"

He says this in English, his voice more serious than she might have expected.

"May I have another daiquiri?" she asks, beginning to enjoy the effects of the first.

"*Yofi*," great. "Anything you like."

Looking pleased with himself, he summons the waiter with a downward wave of his paint-stained hands. His red belly peeks out from beneath the dislodged beach towel.

"Has anyone ever told you how much you resemble Titian's Venus?" he says.

She clucks her tongue, giddy and not caring anymore who might be listening.

"I think I'm drunk."

"That's entirely appropriate." He reaches over and gently kneads her shoulder muscles. "You're on vacation. Relax."

She stiffens.

"Relax," he coaxes.

"Is this how it's done?" she says woozily. "I mean, people come to these places and get friendly and whatever else…I ask, you see, because I've always been married. There's only been my husband."

"No formula for these things. If the chemistry happens—well, one is human."

His hands continue to knead, gradually inching downward.

"Not here," she whispers, and starts to giggle.

"My room's not far."

He steers her by an arm, drawing her closer each time she stumbles. At the end of a corridor, he opens a door and nudges her forward. His hotel room, identical to hers, contains a king-sized bed and little else. She feels him pull her hair to one side and suckle at the nape of her neck. His breath smells of tobacco and fermented fruit.

"Relax," he says, pressing himself against her haunches like a slab of half-cooked beef.

There's a term for this, she thinks: *a coupling as of animals, a bodily function, devoid of any higher impetus.* Queasy, she topples onto the bed with the stranger dead weight atop her.

"That's a good girl…" he murmurs, slurring the words.

Breaking free, she turns to face him.

"You've not told me your name."

"Seymour."

"Well, Seymour, my friend," she says, holding him at arm's length with the sobriety of her gaze, "I know when I've made an ass of myself. I shouldn't have come."

His pluck falls away. "Damn right."

# # #

Leah unpacks her overnight bag, assailed by empty space, by distance and memories. Her trench coat smells of seashells. She didn't take the time to shower, having fled Eilat with sand in her shoes and the alcohol from three pineapple daiquiris still fogging her thoughts. Seymour, a decent sort in the end, insisted on buying her a cup of black coffee. Night had fallen by the time she reached Jerusalem. She had parked in the garage and proceeded in all haste for her apartment, wanting nothing more than to close a door behind her.

She catches sight of herself in the dresser mirror. Her eyes look bloodshot and the tip of her nose has begun to peel. On an impulse, she tears the top sheet from the bed and drapes it across the offending glass; she draws the curtains.

Replacing her rubber beach shoes with the homey pink slippers, she pads to the telephone and retrieves the messages from her answering machine. Her mother, bedridden with bursitis. A client, seized by panic and ranting about avenging angels. A telemarketer, selling something she has no use for.

Listless as lint, she drifts through the silent rooms.

At the threshold of Jacob's study, she pauses. Her husband has left behind a favorite sweater and the one surviving photograph of his mother. The memo he had been drafting the morning of his departure has blown onto the carpet. Unable to take another step, she sinks into the desk chair, its upholstery still bearing the imprint of Jacob's meager buttocks. She lays her head on the blotter and closes her eyes.

"Asleep?" she hears a familiar voice ask.

Bolting upright, she swivels to find her husband standing in the doorway, dressed in a suit too warm for the climate and holding a briefcase.

"I knocked…" He sounds apologetic. "I came as soon as I heard." Getting no response, he inquires anxiously, "Have you seen Dov?"

"Let me get you a cup of tea."

She walks past him and into the kitchen, comforted by the sound of his footfalls still in synch with her own. Keeping her back to him, she puts the kettle on.

"He looks well. Normal. Our Dov."

"Normal?"

"Like a soldier. Only they've got him washing dishes."

Jacob, his jaw unclenching by degrees, leans sighing against the doorframe.

"Before this is over, there'll be more like him."

"Before this is over," she rejoins, vaguely aware of having heard the line before, "we won't know our own children."

"Dov has always been a rebel."

"No, just our son."

"And you?" Jacob says. "How are you doing?"

She half turns, far enough to glance at his face, which looks drawn and could use a shave.

"Fine."

He lingers in the entryway like an uninvited guest waiting to be asked in.

"Sit," Leah says.

Loosening his tie, he takes his old place at the head of the table.

"I'll make some phone calls first thing tomorrow morning, see about getting Dov posted within the Green Line once he's done his time."

"That's settled, then."

She serves him a cup of dark tea with a sprig of fresh mint.

"The Arab woman doesn't come anymore." She returns to the cupboard for a tin of biscuits. "I saw her son on the cover of

Ha'Aretz—arrested, maybe deported by now."

"What did he do?"

"He and a friend were making homemade bombs; blew his own arm off."

Jacob only shakes his head.

"So?" Leah takes a seat beside him.

"Nice tan."

"Oh, *that*."

She would like to say, enough already, we're too old, too accustomed to each other, to lead separate lives. Instead she turns her face away and blurts, "I'll give you a divorce, if that's what you want."

Jacob winces.

"Who said anything about a divorce?"

"You love her, don't you?"

"Yes—no—what does it matter? She's unknowable." He takes his forehead into his hands, the brow furrowed, confusion written there in a hundred intersecting creases. "Ludicrous, wasn't it—losing my head over a poem? A *poem*, and a woman who never comes down to earth long enough to be anything but a stranger."

"Then you didn't…the two of you weren't…?"

"No."

They stare past each other, measuring distances.

"Look, we're both tired," he says finally. "Why don't we talk in the morning?"

"You're welcome to stay."

"In the boys' room?"

"Who said anything about the boys' room?"

Leah awakens with a tremor at her core, the nightmare receding into morning's first light. She feels the chill of another summer ending; already the songbirds have begun their migration south.

"That same dream?" Jacob asks drowsily, reaching out a hand to anchor her.

"Go back to sleep," she tells him.

Gathering herself in like a harvest of salt, Leah brushes her lips across her husband's stubbly cheek, rises from bed, and makes her way to the kitchen. Her sons have come home for *Shabbat*. Today her table will be full.

PALESTINE

Sana Mahmoud knows what it's like to be locked in, locked out, and left on the sidewalk with nothing but her trademark cashmere cardigan and a pocket comb.

Every few weeks since the *Intifada* erupted, one or another shit-talking Israeli in uniform has padlocked and welded shut the front door of her orphanage. The smart ones weld the rear and side doors as well. She has grown accustomed to entering and exiting through the bathroom window, which is low to the ground and obscured by an overgrown honeysuckle bush.

"When the Jews padlock the windows, I'll use the skylight," she vows to the children, whose lives she tends like thirsty saplings planted in sand.

Sana has run the orphanage from the time she was widowed. Her husband fell during the War of '67 while attempting to erect a Palestinian flag on the grounds of the Knesset. It was an utterly futile act but a glorious death, one her people held up as an example and never forgot. Sana, having by that time ceased to love the man whose infidelities she tolerated but whose lack of discretion she never forgave, was less impressed. Widowhood came as a relief. Funds flowed into Sana's hands from unnamed sources—and with them the mission that would fulfill her as no man could. She would give a home to children orphaned by the struggle. She would raise the next generation of Palestinian nationalists.

Today the authorities have sent a dumb soldier, so only the front door has been sealed shut.

Sana leads the orphans through the service entrance into the courtyard. Forced to reside indoors like house cats, they've grown skittish. Talking in whispers, their eyes narrowed to slits, they gather fallen almonds and stray bits of colored glass. The young ones, encouraged by Sana, scoop up dirt with their tiny hands.

"Land," she tells them, "is the mother. When the Jews took away our fields and our groves, they made orphans of us all."

"They took my grandfather's house," laments a cross-eyed boy in patent leather shoes.

Says another, "They took our whole village."

"The Zionists won't be happy," Sana intones with arms outstretched like well-pruned branches, "until they've stolen our last lemon tree. That is their nature."

Stifling a sigh, she surveys the untended grounds. The gardener, rendered stone by the death of his only son, hasn't come to work since Ramadan. The flowerbeds languish choked by weeds.

She turns to an anemic-looking young woman, her niece Amal, and taking her by the arm, seeks shade beneath the termite-ravaged roof of a leaning gazebo.

"I received another fax from Tunis," she says in a voice thinned by age and too many sleepless nights. "The Old Man is sending a friend in need of a few days' hospitality." The young woman nods knowingly. "No one must suspect anything." Sana's tired eyes scan the hedgerow. "You'll put the children to bed early tonight and send the housekeeper home. I'll prepare the guest quarters myself."

"One of the boys discovered the stairway, Aunt. I told him it led to a root cellar full of rats and scorpions—that should fix his curiosity."

The orphanage, a mansion from the Ottoman era that once housed an eccentric sultan, contains a subterranean chamber ingeniously concealed behind a panel of carved ivory.

Sana came upon it by chance one day while directing an exterminator to a hornet's nest. The cell had been littered with skulls. Since the occupation, it has—on more than one occasion—served as a refuge for PLO functionaries needing to get in or out of Israel without calling attention to themselves. Sana has furnished it with a bed, a vanity table, a desk, and a porcelain potty.

Of her latest house guest, Sana knows nothing. Her instructions are to provide a change of clothing and vegetarian meals. She has learned to ask no questions of the Old Man, whose very life has become an endless bout of secrecy and subterfuge.

"The children mustn't suspect anything," Sana says, gazing in their direction. "Neither must the Jews. The guest will arrive in the plumber's truck—if anyone asks, tell them the sinks are backing up again."

Amal runs colorless hands through her lank black hair. Sana's nineteen-year-old protégé, already labeled an old maid by those who see in her plainness and feminist rhetoric insurmountable liabilities, has taken to the life of the orphanage like a hen to straw. She keeps a head count of the children, sees that their clothes are laundered and their lessons memorized.

"One more thing: I'll need a man's suit."

"Any particular size?"

Her instructions hadn't specified and she hadn't dared inquire after such trifles.

"One of my husband's will be fine. Just take the mothballs out of the pockets."

Sana leads the plumber and *his assistant*, duly disguised in coveralls, through the service entrance into a windowless foyer illumined by a single kerosene lamp.

"Why so late?" She motions her visitors toward two brocade chairs with mended upholstery.

"Flat tire," the tradesman replies, absently twisting the worry beads in his chafed hands. "The streets are full of stones and glass. *Ma'lish*," could be worse.

Sana steals a look at her mysterious guest, who is shorter than she might have expected and clean-shaven. A cap obscures the stranger's eyes and casts the rest of his face into shadow.

"You must be hungry," Sana says.

"I have no appetite," the guest responds in a tired voice. "A place to sleep is all that's needed."

Sana, dissembling her disappointment, gestures toward the door. "My apologies for the humble accommodations. Their location ensures privacy but affords no view whatsoever, I'm afraid."

The guest, head drooping as if weighted down by lead fetters, plods ahead.

"I'll stay a while longer," says the plumber, "in case the Jews are watching the entrance."

Sana gives an approving nod.

Holding aloft the lamp, she overtakes the stranger and leads him through a labyrinth of corridors and down a crumbling stone staircase. The musty odor in this part of the house suggests decomposition—centuries of it. Sana has unearthed rat corpses with the heel of her pumps. She treads gingerly.

"Watch your step." She steers the guest by an elbow, brushes low-lying cobwebs from the door frames.

Where the corridor dead-ends, she puts down the lamp and stands facing the carved ivory panel. Her hands palpate its scrolled border.

"There's a hidden latch," she explains, "very high-tech for an era when donkeys moved the city and sewage flowed through the streets."

The panel gives way. Sana retrieves the lamp and leads the guest across the threshold into an irregularly shaped room—closer to a hexagon than a square—with dark stone walls.

"No frills. Help yourself to whatever's here: matches, a spare toothbrush, writing paper...I believe you'll find the bed quite comfortable."

Yawning, the guest drops into the desk chair and hunches forward onto his elbows.

"I won't wake you tomorrow. There's a buzzer." She points toward the far corner. "Should you want anything, just ring."

"*Shukran*," the stranger says without turning to face her.

"No need to thank me."

His voice fades to a murmur: "In Palestine we will all sleep on beds of rose petals."

Sana grits her teeth as an Israeli soldier backs his jeep into the last of her wisteria bushes.

"Look at them," she says to Amal. "Trampling flowers, spitting everywhere, their uniforms all baggy and unpressed. If these are the chosen people, then I'm the Queen of Sheba."

Amal, joining her aunt at the window, clucks her tongue.

"Do you think they suspect anything?"

"Since when have the Jews needed an excuse to harass us?" Sana huffs, raising her chin in the air. She hasn't slept, having spent the night drafting petitions, which never fails to put her in a foul temper. "Have the children finished breakfast?"

"Yes, Aunt."

"Beds made?"

"Yes, Aunt."

"Remind me to send the Swiss a thank-you note for the new blankets."

A buzzer sounds, bringing Sana to attention with knee-jerk

celerity.

"Our guest. Up early considering his sorry state last night. Quickly, niece, the breakfast tray."

"Shall I bring the suit?" Amal asks en route to the door.

"By all means. He arrived without a single item of luggage—not even a wallet, from what I could see. I'd better take him a razor."

Sana assembles her cargo and sets off for the underground chamber. The fatigue of moments ago has vanished; in its place, anticipation surges like rainwater in a wadi. She wonders about her guest, if he has slept, dreamed, awakened lonely or sad or grimly determined. Perhaps he will want to talk, as travelers sometimes do.

She finds the ivory panel ajar.

"I couldn't resist fiddling with it," the guest says in explanation. He stands awkwardly in the middle of the cell with his cap still on and a vacant expression on his half-hidden face. "Is it morning?"

Sana sets down the tray and drapes the suit across a chairback.

"A sunny morning." She strains to infuse the words with light.

"In Palestine every room will have a window."

"*Inshallah.*"

Sana, feeling the gloom overtake her by degrees, focuses on the mundane task at hand.

"I've brought you some breakfast, today's *Al Quds*, a change of clothes, some shaving things. What more might you be needing?"

"Do you have a curling iron?" the guest asks in a tone of apology. "It's vain of me, I know."

Sana dissembles her surprise.

"A curling iron? I'll check upstairs."

"And panties, if you can spare them."

"Excuse me?" Sana clamps hands to her hips in an eloquent declaration of gravity. "What do you think I'm running here, a bordello? I'll not tolerate such—" The guest, starting toward her, blurts, "I'm

96

not what you think I am."

He yanks the cap from his head, loosing a cascade of long black hair. He tears open the buttoned front of his coveralls and steps out of them, revealing the delicate figure of a young woman clad in nothing but a brassiere and nylon half slip.

Sana can only mutter, "Why didn't they tell me?"

The girl huddles against the wall, shivering with cold and crying through haunted eyes. Sana seizes the blanket from the bed and drapes it about her bare shoulders.

"Hush now, the worst has passed."

Sana's latest instructions, received by fax from Tunis that after-noon, read only, *Keep guest comfortable. Transport will be arranged.*

She has taken the girl one of Amal's dresses, a small bottle of Chanel No. 22, a mirror and the curling iron, and found her lying listlessly on the bed, staring into the flame of a dying candle.

"What shall I call you, child?"

"I used to be called Yasmin, but she doesn't exist anymore. Give me any name you like."

Sana spends the rest of the day engaged only superficially in the routinized care of the orphans. Between history lessons and haircuts, her mind wanders to the nameless young woman. She wonders where she's come from, what she's fleeing, and why the Old Man would take a personal interest in her plight. She analyzes the girl's smallest ges-ture, searching for a clue. The studious correctness of her speech sug-gests exile, a Western education. Her grooming and manners suggest wealth. Sana runs down a mental checklist of prominent Palestinian families, but can't place her.

At six p.m. sharp she heaps a platter with yogurt, bread, and fresh figs, runs a comb through her graying hair, and heads for the staircase. Through the kitchen window she glimpses the sunset and a waiting sliver of moon, then darkness closes in, stranding her midway to her destination. Willing herself calm though a thousand demons lurk in her path, she sets down the tray and lights the lamp.

She finds the guest dressed and perfumed, pacing barefoot from wall to wall with an open book in her hand.

"Reading?"

"Simone de Beauvoir—*The Second Sex*. I found it beside the bed."

"I keep it there to educate our brothers in the struggle," Sana says with inflated irony. "They mustn't imagine that women will still be washing their feet once liberation comes."

The guest winces.

"I shall call you Simone," Sana hastens to add, "if that suits you."

The younger woman, apparently pleased with the alias, hugs the book to her chest. Sana busies herself arranging the meal.

"Are you managing to sleep?"

"I do little else," the girl says flatly. Then, pleading, "When will they come for me? I can't stay here."

"Don't worry. Tunis is working on it."

Sana, straining to project a confidence she herself has ceased to feel, empties the platter and turns to go.

"Anything else you'd like?"

The girl collapses onto the bed with limbs askew.

"Wings," she murmurs.

Sana awakens fully dressed, having fallen asleep at her desk to the drone of Radio Monte Carlo.

"It's really too odd, Aunt," Amal says. Switching off the reading lamp, she points in the direction of a rear window. "There's a woman in the courtyard, a crazy woman running in circles. She has no shoes on."

Trailing a woolen afghan behind her, Sana pads drowsily across the carpet and looks out. In the low light of dawn the guest jogs along the perimeter of the hedgerow with a graceful, athletic stride.

"If I didn't know better," Amal ventures, "I would swear she's wearing my dress."

"That foolish willful girl! Draw all the curtains. Fetch me a pad-lock."

"What shall I tell the children?"

"Nothing."

Smoothing her skirt with a downward sweep of the hand, Sana walks briskly out the service entrance and into the courtyard. She glances toward the street, surveys the neighboring rooftops; nothing stirs. Relieved but taking no chances, she steps into the girl's path and squares her stance.

"Time's up, Simone."

The girl's expression contracts, her stride lengthens. Still run-ning, she sidesteps Sana and heads for the entrance, long hair tossing wildly in her wake.

"I know the way," she calls back.

Sana, her gait heavy, follows at a distance. At the threshold of the chamber, she takes the errant guest by both shoulders and studies her face.

"What's come over you? I won't have you placing the orphanage—everything we've worked for—in danger for the sake of your reckless pleasure."

"Pleasure?" the girl echoes bitterly.

Sana appropriates the Prophet's rebuke: "*Did you think to enter par-adise without suffering the violence of those who have come before you?*"

Simone hangs her head. Sana stands trembling, silent, shackled by her own thoughts. At eye level a spider spins its web.

"I'm not supposed to talk, you know," the guest emits in a choked whisper. "That's the price of my rescue—never to tell my story."

Sana waves a scrolled fax transmission in the air, snarling, "Those paper-pushers in Tunis are useless. They bluster and issue proclamations, but when it comes to getting anything done, they blow smoke. In the end it's all up to us on the inside." Handing the paper to Amal, she says, "Look at this. They can't even figure out how to get the guest across the border. The Old Man says they can't spare the manpower."

"*Suggest you use decoy,*" Amal reads aloud.

"A brilliant tactic. Bravo! Nothing we haven't done before. Decoy out the front door, guest out the back, and with any luck the Jews running in circles just long enough for us to get her out of Jerusalem. But who'll be the goose—that's the question."

The young woman takes the matron by the sleeve of her cardigan and leads her to a crushed velvet windowseat overlooking the waste-land of a garden.

"Why not me?"

"A well-bred Palestinian woman traveling alone?" Sana punctuates her displeasure with an upward toss of the chin. "It's not done. And besides, your parents would never agree to it, desperate as they are to marry you off to some achingly proper sheik."

"Oh really, Aunt—"

"A foreign woman would arouse less suspicion," Sana goes on, "one of these tourists walking the streets like a pack animal. But then, why would one of them help us? Who could we trust?"

"I know someone."

Sana drums her fingers on the armrest.

"Have you heard of Eve?"

"Eve...why does that name sound familiar? Not that American? The Jewess? The one your brother Salim made such a scandal with and then unloaded like a used car. I wonder how she's taking the news of Salim's marriage."

"How would any woman feel in her place?"

"How naive you are, niece. Haven't you heard the latest news?" She cups a hand to the side of her mouth. "The United Jewish Appeal is sending young women infected with the AIDS virus to Jerusalem. Like a secret weapon."

Amal's lower lip drops open.

"How *is* Salim?" Sana adds as an afterthought.

"In good health, but Mama worries about him. He's started reading self-help books."

"He'll get over it, once his in-laws loosen up on the purse strings." She makes no attempt to conceal her disdain for Salim, whose materialism and lack of political conscience have long peeved her. His defection to Amman—and a life of aimless affluence—had surprised no one, Sana least of all. "Remind me to drop our cousins a note. Surely they can spare a computer or two for the children."

A sudden wind wafts the now familiar bite of tear gas through the open window.

Wrinkling her nose, she says, "We'd best get the children to bed. But tell me, what do you know about this Eve?"

"She resembles Simone," her niece replies. "I've seen a photograph—Salim kept it hidden in his cufflink box."

Sana, her patience at an end, rejoins brusquely, "What are her politics? What is she doing in Jerusalem? Why would she help us?"

"She believes in justice; I can tell from the poems she writes."

"Words."

"Her love for Salim was more than words."

"She fell for his Middle Eastern charm, like dozens of other tourists. The sociology books call it the Canadian Secretary Syndrome. It means nothing."

Amal stoops to brush a speck of dust from her blunt-toed shoes.

"That may be," she says in a shrinking voice. "But Salim has left, and Eve has stayed."

Sana concedes with a half-shrug.

"I'll talk to her."

The hum of children's voices warms an unseasonably cool morning. Sana, buttoning her cardigan, searches the casements for the source of a draft. Through a breach in the curtains, she catches sight of three cars with yellow license plates pulling up to the front curb.

From the first car emerges an acquaintance from the Israeli peace camp, conspicuous as a storm in her threadbare purple ski pants and fuchsia poncho and carrying a placard lettered in English, *End the Occupation!* The rest of the demonstrators, barely more presentable, clamber out of the vehicles and assemble in a snaking line along the sidewalk.

"The hippies are back," Sana calls across the room to her niece. "Take them some tea. Wait, I'll go with you."

Sana tugs the hem of her classic black skirt down over her knees and pins a pearl brooch to her blouse collar. She inspects her hands for ink stains.

"Use the silver platter, but not the good china. There should be some Styrofoam cups left from the march."

The children, quick to detect the slightest disturbance on the street, have gathered at the windows.

"The *jaysch* are coming!" cries a young girl in a ruffled pinafore.

"No, not the soldiers," one of the older children hastens to correct her. "These are the good Jews."

Says the cross-eyed boy, "There are no good Jews."

Sana orders the curtains drawn shut. Closing the bathroom door behind her, she hefts her middle-aged bulk onto the sill and out the window and lands with a crunching sound in a bed of dead roses. Brushing pollen and desiccated leaves from her sweater, she reaches out a hand for the tea service.

"We're low on sugar," Amal remarks.

"This isn't the Inter-Continental."

With a brisk and unabashedly mannish stride Sana plots a course toward the demonstrators, who, marching in no particular formation, have begun to chant in Hebrew.

Amal treads on her heels. "What are they saying, Aunt?"

"The usual patter. They might as well be hawking peanuts, for all the difference it makes."

She approaches the remains of the front lawn and, redoubling her guard, takes stock of the situation. The soldiers have retreated to the opposite street corner. A barrel-chested commander of modest stature paces the length of the jeep with a walkie-talkie pressed to one ear.

"We don't have long. They're probably calling for reinforcements." She hands her niece the tray. "You go," she directs, then pointing with her chin toward the officer adds, "I'll keep an eye on shorty."

Her niece hesitates, riveted by the figure of a dark woman, smartly if simply dressed, who stands apart from the others with face upturned and eyes hidden behind a pair of tortoiseshell sunglasses.

"It's *Eve*," Amal whispers. "She looks like the photograph, only older."

Sana, reserving comment, studies her. Eve doesn't resemble the

Americans she's known, with their gaudy clothes and exaggerated cheerfulness. She appears pensive, vaguely Semitic, and her carriage suggests an innate dignity. As Sana watches her, Eve ventures closer to the demonstration, evincing no sign of fear or reticence.

"A poet, you said she was?"

"I pictured her taller."

An armored truck rounds the corner. Soldiers scramble down its flanks and converge on the demonstrators in hive-like disarray.

"And not one television camera!" Sana laments with contained fury, stamping a heel into the parched clods of ruined grass. Then, serene as ice, "Never mind, just get Eve. I'll be in my office."

The demonstrators disperse with only token resistance and head for their cars. From her office window, Sana hears a soldier left behind on guard duty curse in Arabic as he spits sunflower seed husks onto her front steps.

Seized by melancholy, she remembers her husband's voice, not the soft earnest voice he used to court her but the angry voice, the one that came later, once he started to drink. He'd been a newspaper columnist, popular while his Pan-Arabist rhetoric held sway among the Palestinian elite. Slow to embrace the militant nationalism of the PLO, he lost his public, his influence, and with these things some vital part of himself. He took a mistress, then another. He grew a rakish little mustache like Omar Sharif's. While Sana lay flat on her back for nine months with a bad pregnancy, he flew off to Paris with his latest bottle blonde. Their child dropped into the world stillborn, a wizened baby boy with dead eyes.

"Just as well," her husband had muttered at the burial, "the Jews would only have made a lackey of him."

"Aunt?"

She turns to find Amal standing at attention in the doorway, Eve beside her looking no less of an enigma without her dark glasses.

"Welcome to Palestine," she greets the American, motioning toward the one chair not covered with primers or folded handkerchiefs.

Eve, nodding a silent greeting, seats herself.

"Will you take tea?"

"Please don't bother."

Sana takes her place behind the desk.

"Cigarette?"

"No, thank you."

Abandoning protocol, Sana stares straight into Eve's eyes and says, "I didn't think you'd come. Do you know who I am?"

"Everyone knows who you are."

"And everyone is wrong. The Israelis think I'm a radical inciting children to violence. The old guard calls me a man-hating feminist. It's even been rumored that I was once Arafat's mistress." She raises her chin to an even more imperious angle and brings both hands to her heart. "I'm a Palestinian, that's all."

"And a Mahmoud."

"Elitist, you mean?" she rejoins with mock offense. "My name isn't the asset you might imagine. Admittedly, I have certain...connections, shall we say?"

"What is this about?" Eve interjects.

Her tone remains cordial, but beneath it Sana senses a growing disquiet.

"Close the door," she directs her niece. Lighting a filterless cigarette, she curls forward until her matronly bosom grazes the desk. "You're too smart a woman to have allowed my nephew to toy with you. The boy has been nothing but an embarrassment. I do apologize."

Eve's sigh is audible.

"My niece tells me you write poetry."

"I dabble."

"We Palestinians are great admirers of poetry. Through the darkest years of our history, Palestine has been kept alive in our imaginations through verse." She swivels toward the window and her lips stiffen. "This street has become ugly. No one comes to collect the garbage. The soldiers drive their jeeps over anything that blooms. But when I close my eyes I can smell the lemon blossoms of my homeland—they're as real to me as that snot-nosed soldier sitting on my doorstep."

Amal steps forward.

"We need your help."

"My help?" Eve raises an eyebrow. "What can I possibly do for you?"

"A small errand," rejoins Sana.

At the far end of the office a stack of newspapers quakes, the topmost sheets scatter, and a muffled sneeze emits through the interstices. Sana and Amal exchange a knowing look.

"Samira," Sana calls with measured sternness, "come out from there."

A little girl wracked by nervous giggles emerges crawling from her hiding place and darts across the room. Taking refuge on Eve's lap, she covers her eyes with two glossy brown pigtails.

"There, there." Eve cradles the girl in her arms. "No need to hide. No one's going to hurt you."

The girl wavers between laughter and tears, clutching at the bodice of Eve's dress with hands that grip, recoil. Eve glances sad-eyed at Sana.

"What's the matter with her?"

Sana signals for Amal to take the child. There's a moment's

pause, as if the three women have locked into an earthly constellation and cannot be separated, as if something larger than any or all of them were being decided. Eve rocks the girl until her feverish body goes still, then surrenders her.

"Wait." Eve unclasps a delicate gold necklace. "I want Samira to have this."

Sana pockets the gift without comment. Amal backs through the door with the girl once more a bundle of twitches in her arms and closes the latch behind them.

"She's been like that for weeks," Sana says bitterly. "Soldiers blew up her house—they claimed her brother had planted bombs, but any pretext will do. Samira's father went on a rampage; when it was over, he killed himself." Sana pauses, watching Eve's eyes cloud over like miniature skies. "Samira saw it all."

"And her mother?"

"The Carmelite sisters are caring for her. She has not been well."

The two women sit without speaking. In the background children's voices drone, reciting by rote Muhammad's parable of the garden. An ancient cuckoo wheezes the noon hour. Already tasting victory, Sana leans across her desk in a posture of invitation.

"Will you have that cup of tea now?"

Weary and triumphant in equal parts, Sana pushes open the ivory panel and calls out a perfunctory greeting to Simone.

"Everything is arranged. You'll leave tomorrow morning for Ben-Gurion Airport and fly nonstop to New York." She places a weathered rucksack on the desk. "Tickets, passport, blue jeans…You speak English, I understand?"

"Tomorrow." The girl smiles for the first time since her arrival at the orphanage. "Then, they've called my mother?"

"Tunis assures me that someone will be waiting for you at the other end."

Simone rifles through the luggage and extracts a pair of athletic shoes.

"Size six and a half," Sana says mechanically.

"The first thing I'm going to do when I get home is jog from one end of the city to the other."

"Home?"

"I grew up in the States, didn't they tell you?"

Sana perches on the edge of the desk and levels her gaze on the girl whose name has expired and whose story has been sold cut-rate like damaged goods.

"I would have liked to know you."

The girl drops to her knees before the matron and lays her head in the tailored lap. Sana, transfigured by pity into the mother she might have been, extends a hand toward the thick plaits of black hair.

"Speak, child. They haven't bought your soul."

Simone sits back on her haunches.

"You've heard of Khadija Kanafani, my mother?"

Sana nods, remembering a quiet raven-haired schoolmate from Bir Zeit University who had married beneath her station, languished in a village somewhere near Jericho, and then—amid rumors of domestic violence and disgrace—disappeared altogether.

"I wondered what became of her."

"When I was three, she left my father and took me to live in White Plains, New York. She teaches Comparative Lit there."

Straining her memory, Sana asks, "Weren't there sons?"

"My brothers, Latif and Fayek. They stayed with my father."

"What brought you back? You must have had a good life in America."

"An easy life, sure. But I dreamed of Palestine. I couldn't understand how my mother, having seen with her own eyes how our people were tricked out of their land, could abandon the struggle. I blamed her for breaking up our family. I imagined my father and brothers in Jericho, the hardships they were enduring under occupation while I lived a frivolous life. When my older brother wrote me a letter hinting at certain covert operations he'd had a hand in, I vowed to get back here any way I could. In my freshman year at Bryn Mawr, I used my scholarship money to buy a plane ticket. I returned to our village burning with revolutionary zeal, parroting slogans, ready for any sacrifice…No one knew what to make of me. I'd become an outsider, like my mother. The Palestine I'd risked everything for, where the water ran sweet and we'd all be of one heart—what had it been but *hype?*"

"No, a vision. Something worth striving for."

"That's what I once believed." Simone traces jagged boundaries on her thighs with a clenched fist. "I enrolled at Bir Zeit, became an activist. A group of us forged alliances with students on the Israeli Left—communists, mostly. There was one guy, David Perach, who seemed a little different from the others. He wasn't full of hot air like some, who'd talk about peace and then report for army duty in the occupied territories; David lived his politics. I could talk to him. I thought of him as a friend."

She looks down, as if having lost something.

"A rumor started in the village, saying that I was sleeping with him. They figured since I'd grown up in the States, I must be loose anyway. My brothers caught wind of it."

"They made trouble?"

"They stabbed my friend—left him to bleed to death in a public toilet."

Sana, having heard too many stories to be shocked or outraged, only sighs.

"The Jews are looking for me," the girl goes on, her American accent growing more pronounced, "for questioning."

"And your brothers?"

"Gone into hiding, in the caves outside al-Uja."

"So, you're fleeing the authorities?"

The young woman's head drops lower.

"No, I'm running from my own father. He's sworn to kill me."

"Oh, child. Oh, my poor Yasmin…" Sana sinks onto her knees and embraces the girl. "These are things of the past, brutish things. I see the future in you, Yasmin. Come back to us one day."

Sana strips the linen from the brass bed and blows out the candle. She pulls shut the ivory panel, sealing off the empty chamber with its suggestive odors and its ghosts. As she ascends the staircase, emerging through the dimness into the low-hanging smog of a Jerusalem afternoon, she has the urge to weep. Her dreams seem so far away, the walls so high.

In the foyer she drops the laundry into a hamper and reminds herself to send Amal for soap flakes. Her cardigan has lost a button. She's had no lunch. Spent, she leans against the doorframe and closes her eyes.

On the other side of the door the orphans' voices burst into song and reverberate off the crumbling roof beams. Transported by the sound to a place where history casts no shadow, she feels her heart lift. To Palestine, land of fragrant orchards and laughter. To Palestine, ewes grazing beneath an impossibly blue sky and the children skipping off to school in freshly laundered uniforms…

Home at last, she steps out into the light and feels a southerly breeze waft over her like the caress of Allah's own hand.

THE FIRST HARVEST

J acob Halevi knew he was destined for great things the night he first sat down in David Ben-Gurion's red rocking chair with a hardcover book in his lap and rocked to the sound of crickets and Liszt's *Transcendental Etudes*.

Jacob had been thirteen or so, Ben-Gurion ancient beyond reckoning, and Israel both younger and older than either of them. Israel had given both a second life, a chance to make history. Ben-Gurion rose to glory as the state's first Prime Minister, retreated in disillusionment, and rose again. Jacob built a few bridges and bought a condo. He still reads books and listens to classical music, but always with a vague sense of having lost something, of losing by the very act of living. He misses Ben-Gurion. He misses the father he never knew and the mother whose girlish face smiles sadly from a faded sepia photograph.

He doesn't speak of his life before Israel. Having been an infant when the Nazis overran Poland, he had no childhood. This much is known: that his father died in the uprising of the Warsaw Ghetto and his mother at Auschwitz, that Jacob escaped to the countryside and spent the remainder of the War years foraging in the gardens of peasants and sleeping in their stables. An American soldier found him after the Armistice. He had improvised shoes from horses' feedbags and wandered into the capital with an empty potato sack slung across a shoulder and his mother's portrait sewn into his shirt. Efforts were made to reunite him with relatives, but none had survived.

A succession of refugee camps gave him a toehold in the world until the Jewish Agency put him on a ship bound for Haifa. It was the winter of 1948 and everyone in Israel, it seemed, had just arrived. They were lean, most of them, they had nothing, but their eyes shone with hope.

Five years later, bearing a new name and speaking a new language, he arrived at Kibbutz Sde Boker. A sunburnt kibbutznik in khaki shorts greeted him at the gate with a resounding "*Shalom!*" and a hug so avid that it fractured one of his ribs.

When it rains he swears he can feel the wound still, like a pinprick in his side, reminding him of having found his way home and then lost the key.

Jacob awakens with a start, his wife, Leah, beside him gasping, "Don't, not my son..." from the depths of a tormented sleep.

Her nightmares have become as real to him as the pillow beneath his head. They began with the birth of Amnon, a first son fated to become a soldier by the mere fact of his having been born Israeli. Jacob too is a soldier, a reservist now, though he has never thought of himself as one. His uniforms don't fit. They seem to belong to someone else, someone brawnier, of more heroic proportions. When he was decorated for valor after the Yom Kippur War, he went back to his condo, locked himself in the bedroom, and cried—not for the dead but for the living, who by killing had cleft their own hearts.

"Which one was it this time, Amnon or Dov?" he asks mechanically, reaching out a tired hand to wipe the tears from his wife's cheek.

"Go back to bed," she murmurs.

He watches her sit up and gather her unruly auburn hair into a ponytail. If he ignores the gray streaks at her temples and the worry lines beside her mouth, she might be the girl whose swaying walk once drew him racing across the orchards of Sde Boker for the bitter pleasure of watching her pass. Unlike the other girls at the kibbutz, for whom he felt a familial affection, Leah never greeted him or returned his glances. Her aloofness gave her an air of exoticism, it freed him to imagine her naked, and finally to court her.

"It's the Sabbath," he whispers, taking her by the shoulders and gently tugging her back.

"But the boys are home. They'll be up soon, and hungry."

"They're old enough to get their own breakfast."

He begins to undo the buttons on her combed cotton pajama top, stops midway and burrows through the surplus fabric to her breasts.

"You're more beautiful than ever," he says, lying, but believing it somehow.

Jacob, fresh from a shower, his face randomly dotted with vestiges of shaving cream, pads, self-conscious, into the kitchen. His sons, Amnon and Dov, slouch over the previous day's newspapers, quietly swapping headlines between sips of cocoa and mouthfuls of dry granola.

"*Boker tov*," he murmurs, unsure whether to kiss them or clap them on the back or simply take his accustomed seat and wait to be absorbed into their conversation.

Such quandaries plague Jacob constantly. When his sons were small, the role of father had been easier, his choices fewer and more clear-cut. He had provided, changed the occasional diaper. Leah had done the rest. His sons might resemble him, but in character they are their mother's creation, tougher than Jacob, less prone to brood.

"Maccabi got trounced again." Dov pushes the sports section across the cluttered tabletop.

Adds Amnon with the same nonchalance, "Their power forward was nabbed on drug charges."

"Not to worry," quips Dov, "he's good on the rebound."

Jacob glances at the newspaper without interest.

"Save room for your mother's waffles. You know how she loves to fuss over *Shabbat* meals."

"I'll set the table," Amnon volunteers, beginning to push back his chair.

Leah strides into the room with her habitual air of purpose. "Sit, relax." Seizing command, she proceeds to assemble an ambitious array of boxes and jars on the kitchen counter. She has washed her hair and wrapped it in a bath towel. A linen dress Jacob has never seen before drapes softly across her slender figure, stopping just short of the knee. She moves soundlessly, barefooted, as she used to on the kibbutz when preparing meals in the spartan cafeteria.

"Do you remember the first tomatoes we raised at Sde Boker?" he asks, the memory of them suddenly so vivid he can smell their earthy fragrance.

Leah, already pouring batter into the waffle iron, glances at him over a shoulder.

"Puny harvest."

"But the flavor—the wonder of having raised them at all!" he rejoins with contained fervor. "I've never tasted anything like them since."

Leah opens the cutlery drawer and counts out four forks, four teaspoons.

"My mother's bursitis is acting up again. The work committee retired her from the garden and gave her some contrived little clerical job. I've been meaning to pay her a visit."

Jacob hasn't returned to Sde Boker since Ben-Gurion's death. With the old statesman gone and his cottage converted to a museum, the once forward-looking kibbutz shifted its sights to the past. As Ben-Gurion's legacy fell static in archives and memorials, a free-floating lassitude overtook his disciples. The desert sun bleached their convictions a pale shade of yesterday. When Jacob last visited, Leah's mother took him aside on the pretext of asking his advice on the location of a new well.

"You were our hope, *Yaacov*," she said in the flat, perpetually thirsty voice that has come to characterize her widowhood, "the first to go to university, and the first to abandon us."

She knelt then and pressed her hands into the parched soil, a monument to sacrifice and human limitation. Jacob didn't defend himself. He hadn't the heart to tell his mother-in-law that it was Leah who lured him away from the kibbutz, Leah who drove him to seek his fortune in the city. Leaving Sde Boker was the price he paid to have her. Her *ransom*, she had called it.

Leah takes a seat beside him. The scent of her damp hair arouses a residue of desire not quite spent.

"Eat." She pinches the meager flesh at his waist. "You're thin as an Ethiopian, bones all poking out."

Jacob drives south, relaxing by degrees as the landscape thins and the sky widens to crown the horizon. Beside him Leah sits at attention, eyes flitting from one side of the road to the other.

"Wouldn't surprise me if they've added another checkpoint or two since I last passed this way," she says. "Bethlehem's gotten bad. You'd better go fast when we get near the refugee camp."

Jacob turns on the radio, hoping to distract her. He's taken the day off from work, a rare deviation from routine, and he'd like to enjoy the scenery, maybe stop for a picnic lunch. He's wearing an old Panama hat from his college days. With his free hand, he reaches across the car seat and gropes for his wife's breasts.

"Watch the road," she gently scolds him, then dropping the straps of her flowered sundress and swiveling toward him with a decidedly wanton smile, murmurs, "Remember that wadi where we first made love?"

He is about to say, "What an oaf I was," is about to pull her closer, when the first stone grazes the windshield, cracking it through the middle.

"Get down!"

A swarm of children, their faces masked by red and black *kefillahs*, darts along the highway with stones and slingshots in their arms. They are shouting something in Arabic, something nasty-sounding that requires no translation. A second stone strikes the driver's side window, sending splinters of glass into Jacob's cheek. Leah lurches onto his lap, wild-eyed and holding out a revolver.

"Put that away," he snaps.

Grimly focused on the road ahead, he floors the accelerator and doesn't release it until the last angry child has vanished into the distance. He feels his unhealed rib send stitches up his side.

"It's over," Leah reassures him.

Her warm steady fingertips brush glass shards from his shoulders. The tenderness of the gesture breaks down the self-possession that has become his one defense against love and hatred both.

Clasping his wife to him with trembling hands, he blurts, "If anything were to happen to you…"

Dried blood cakes at the corner of his mouth. In Beersheba they stop at a lunch stand and doctor the cuts with ice water and paper napkins.

"We should deport them all, every last one of them," grumbles a dark-skinned man in a greasy apron.

Jacob excuses himself and skulks back to the car.

"Let's not talk about it, *beseder*? Okay? Nothing has happened." He starts the engine and races onto the highway without a backward glance.

# # #

"What am I supposed to tell my mother?" Leah asks as they alight from the car and fall into step on the dusty path to the administration building. "The cracked windshield, your bloody face—what other logical explanation is there?"

"Tell her we were assaulted by a nesting vulture."

She takes his arm.

"Wrong season, and besides, *ima* wouldn't fall for it. She always knows when someone's trying to put something over on her."

Jacob pictures his mother-in-law, her starched lips and work-worn fingers, the *you don't fool me* look that never fails to make him feel unworthy.

"I need a walk," he says. "Why don't I meet you at the house a little later?"

She nods, continues along the path without him. At the doorstep she turns and calls back, "Don't get lost. I want to be on the road before dark."

Ambling with no apparent destination, he retreats to the shade of the date palms. He plucks a ripe fruit and lets it dissolve on his tongue, its sweetness nearly unbearable, like the first throes of love. Tears well in his eyes. The landscape blurs around him. Disoriented and fending off midday languor, he finds himself on the doorstep of Ben-Gurion's cottage. He tries the latch. To his surprise it yields to his touch, admitting him to the familiar parlor, preserved down to the smallest detail—the framed photographs of Ben-Gurion's children and grandchildren, the crocheted doilies, the Lladro figurines, all freshly dusted and occupying their accustomed places. He has a sense of absence, of time trapped within the sun-chastened walls and struggling to break free. Seized by melancholy, he staggers forward into Ben-Gurion's library.

The modest room, lined on all sides by bookshelves that extend from floor to ceiling, arouses in Jacob a longing he can't name. His eyes scan the shelves, they forage, as if the books contained the meaning of life, the grand design behind the trifling mediocrity he's made of things. Mulling over titles—*The Other Side of the River, Dead Souls*, a biography of Mao Tse-tung—he pivots and sees the red rocking chair.

The chair, smaller than he might have remembered it, brings a sob to his throat. He pictures Ben-Gurion seated, rocking, hears him say, *One can't read too many books, Yaacov*. Clinging to the memory like a drowning man to a rock, he drops into the chair and closes his eyes.

"You're not permitted to sit there."

Jacob jars awake to find a weathered old kibbutznik standing over him with one hand on his hip and the other poised on the butt of an automatic rifle.

"Shlomo?" he utters.

"You know me?" The man gives him a guarded look.

"We grew up together."

Jacob shambles to his feet.

"You used to challenge me to arm wrestle. You always won. I was the kibbutz weakling, the kid who never took his face out of a book."

"*Yaacov*, you old pisher!" The man takes Jacob's hand and pumps it like a well handle. "Haven't seen you for years. Heard you made a bundle as an engineer. Who could blame you? Way the world's going."

Jacob studies the man, his leathery face, callused hands, the ill-fitting work clothes, and feels a remote affection sharpened by pity. His former comrade, though no older than himself, looks depleted, as if life has emptied him out and left nothing but this mistreated shell.

"You tripped the alarm," Shlomo says, pointing to a fine expanse of wire.

"I wasn't thinking."

"Oi, *Yaacov*, you haven't changed. Head in the clouds." The kibbutznik takes a frayed handkerchief from his back pocket and wipes the sweat from his forehead. "What happened to your cheek? Cut yourself shaving?"

Jacob's hand rises of its own volition to cup the bruise.

"Slip of the wrist."

Shlomo paces the length of the room, conducting an impromptu inspection.

"Can't be too careful," he says, shaking his head. "How the dead rest anymore, I can't imagine. Ben-Gurion wouldn't have liked the way things are going, that's for certain."

"You mean the trouble with the Arabs?"

"No, the greed. Capitalism. Everyone having to own their own TV, and color yet."

Jacob can only shrug his shoulders.

"Come home with me for a glass of lemonade?" Shlomo says, nudging him toward the door.

"I'll stay here for a while, if that's okay."

Shlomo looks wounded.

"Have it your way. Just don't touch anything or you'll have the whole kibbutz suffering conniptions. They treat this place as if it was the Second Temple."

Jacob hears the front door open and close. He stands in the center of the room, hands pinned to his sides, staring blankly at book bindings.

"I thought I'd find you here."

Leah, come to fetch him. She doesn't enter the library but lingers backlit on the threshold, looking pretty and not so very different from the girl he once made love to in the wadi. It had been his first time. He had fumbled with the buttons on her blouse, gotten dirt in her hair, and felt her belly quiver beneath him like a trapped quail. In the morning he went to her mother and told her they would be married.

"You know me too well," he says, turning his hands palm-up in a gesture of surrender.

"Everyone's asking for you. *Ima* baked you a Black Forest cake. She must think you're mad at her."

Jacob glances toward the rocking chair, reluctant to leave.

"There's something I never told you." He takes a few unsteady steps toward her. They stand for a moment in silence, she indulging him with a rare smile, he nervous and groping for words. "I left this kibbutz because I loved you and couldn't imagine a life without you. I felt like a traitor, and you knew that, yet you led me away. Part of me resented you, thought you'd been selfish. For many years the world outside felt to me like a cold and meaningless place."

"I know," she whispers. "I felt that too."

"Let me finish." He closes the distance between them and looks into her eyes, which are as dark as lodes, unfathomably deep. "I loved you something fierce, and thought that was enough. But as time went on, I began to blame you for the emptiness within myself, for the friendships I didn't have and for the awkwardness I felt around my own sons. Had I stayed on the kibbutz, I told myself, things would have made more sense. I'd *belong*. It was easier to blame you than to face the facts: Israel has changed, and I've become an orphan all over again."

Leah arcs forward and rests her head in the crook of his shoulder. "We're all disheartened."

"Yes, I finally got it." He sinks his fingers into her lavish unbound hair and inhales the scent. "This place, it's not what it once was. We would have been stifled here—but you knew that years ago."

"You had so much talent."

"My head was so full of Ben-Gurion's visions, his impossible ideals. I thought Sde Boker was the beacon that would light up the world."

He begins to laugh, but its hollow sound offends him. *Life is serious business, Yaacov,* he can hear Ben-Gurion chide. The old statesman's presence, palpable still, nudges him in the ribs like a father's gentle reminder.

He wonders aloud, "What will become of our sons?"

"They have choices," Leah murmurs, her breath warm where it meets his neck, "choices we barely dared to dream of. They can study abroad, travel, enter any profession…They can tell Shamir to go to hell. It's up to them now."

Jacob casts a last look at the library and turns to leave.

"Come," Leah says, "I want to show you something."

She leads him out into a breezy afternoon, cool for the season, and with her familiar swaying gait crosses the symmetrical rows of date trees to the greenhouse. Its warped door creaks open on unoiled hinges. Doves perch on the eaves. Stepping out of her shoes, she approaches a potted plant and cups its oversized fruit in the palms of both hands.

"Bumper crop this year," she says, grinning up at him. "Have you ever seen such a Messianic tomato?"

He looks at the perfect red sphere, alive to bursting within its tensile skin, and can't find words to express how happy the sight of it makes him feel, how idiotically exalted.

RESCUE MISSION

Amnon Halevi daydreams about New Zealand, a place he knows virtually nothing about but that in recent years has come to symbolize the peace he's never known. He strains to imagine what it would be like to leave doors unlocked or to buy a loaf of bread without wondering if there's a bomb hidden inside it. Had he been born in New Zealand, he might be saving whales or picking apples instead of poring over files, worrying who the next loony might be.

When someone asks Amnon what he does for a living, he answers in a word: security. His friends know better than to probe for details. Even his own mother can't say for certain what her son does or to whom he reports.

Recruited fresh from a tour of duty in the Israeli Defense Forces, he has the physique for the job if not the emotional armor. His parents had expected him to enroll in a liberal arts college after the army; they'd offered tuition in full, then the further enticement of a summer off to travel and *find himself*, but impelled by some vague notion of patriotism, he decided to put his studies on hold for another year or two. "Until the situation cools down," he tells befuddled friends, who can't understand why someone from an affluent family would rather punch a time clock than fudge term papers.

Rising from his desk chair, he paces the length of his office—eight feet wall to wall—and stretches his hamstrings. Not yet flabby like most of his coworkers, he suffers from a surfeit of pent-up energy.

"Down, Tiger," says Gila, his favorite typist from the clerical pool, as she saunters into his office with the day's quota of overstuffed folders, most stamped *Classified*, the few exceptions relegated to the bottom of the stack. "Shahar's out sick. Good day to sneak an hour at the gym."

"With my luck, Saddam Hussein would bomb Tel Aviv the moment I left."

"Not funny, Halevi."

She lays the files on his desk blotter and backs through the door with the remnant of a smile. Amnon notices the black lace border of her slip peeking out from beneath a short skirt, and wishes he had fewer scruples.

Having been raised by a mother whose iron will shaped his character the way a bulldozer levels mountains, he's learned not to toy with women. The whole of his romantic history can be told on an index card: three girlfriends, all intelligent and good-natured, but whom he couldn't love and couldn't deceive. Since his last relationship gave out, he spends most evenings at the Cinematheque, sometimes with friends, more often alone.

Flexing his calf muscles, he inhales the receding haze of Gila's perfume and rifles through the contents of the topmost file. *Ali Aluba, Gamal* reads the label. Another Arab he's inherited from the Mossad, recently returned from four years at Penn State. The attached buck slip, scrawled in his boss's surly hieroglyphics, cautions, "Keep an eye on him."

He burrows through the pile with waning interest until a Western name catches his eye—*Eve Cavell*. It takes him a moment to connect the name with a face; he's met this woman. An old friend of the family once brought her to his parents' home for *Shabbat*. Her conversation had been hard to follow, its logic dubious, but he still remembers the riotous abundance of her black hair and the innocent, almost childlike way she returned his glances.

"Shit," he utters.

Dropping into his desk chair, he opens the file and begins to read.

"Shit," he says again, shaking his head. "What a mess she's gotten herself into."

The last spokes of sunset fade to gray and vanish into a night sky too steely to harbor a moon. Twitchy in the knees, Amnon stands on line before the box office, waiting to purchase a ticket for Godard's *Contempt*. Distracted for a moment by the poster of Brigitte Bardot draped gloriously nude across virginal white bed sheets, he fails to notice that the queue has advanced and his turn arrived. He begins to extract a five-shekel note from his wallet, then on an impulse pockets it.

"*Slicha*," he says in clipped apology, pressing through the crowd toward the parking lot.

A northerly wind gusts car exhaust and falafel remains along the pavement. Chilled, he turns up the collar of his leather jacket. Glancing over one shoulder and then the other, he slides onto the worn velour seat of his vintage Saab, revs the engine, and heads for the Old City.

As he nears Damascus Gate, traffic thins. Jeep-loads of soldiers—some parked at the curb, others patrolling the surrounding streets—keep a wary eye on the city's Arab population. Leaving his car beneath a street lamp, he makes his way toward the gate, taking care to pull his jacket down low on the hips to cover the bulge of his holster.

"*Laila tov*," he greets the trio of soldiers posted in the archway.

They nod acknowledgment, and one—a Druse, Amnon deduces from the man's accented Hebrew—bums a cigarette.

"Things quiet tonight?"

"Dead," replies the Druse, lighting up with a wooden kitchen match struck against the stone wall.

Amnon hands him the rest of the packet, saying, "Watch it, my friend. That's when some maniac decides to blow up the Temple Mount."

He enters the souk, pausing a moment to allow his eyes to adjust to the darkness, then darts down the winding step street with held breath. There's too little light, too much he can't see and can't guard against. The Via Dolorosa echoes with whispers; old men squat along the shop fronts smoking hookahs, rattling prayer beads. Any one of them might be armed beneath the loose robes. He has seen the *fedayeen* slaughter cows with a four-inch scimitar, head severed, entrails uncoiling like a melee of snakes.

If he were in New Zealand, it would be daytime. He might be riding a bicycle to work or shearing sheep. Perhaps someone would call out a greeting.

The walkway narrows. Swerving to avoid the mangy flanks of a donkey, the sorry creature sagging beneath its cargo of olive oil and green onions, he feels for his pistol. He does this more often than he realizes. To the casual observer, he might appear to be scratching an itch—but there are no casual observers in Jerusalem.

"Shin Bet," whispers a man in a white *kefillah* to his dour-faced neighbor, the pair spitting on the ground in unison as Amnon passes.

A light comes on, illuminating the balcony of number 33 Saffron Street. Amnon, surveying the deserted lane with growing uneasiness, cranes his neck. He catches a fleeting glimpse of Eve's silhouette, drawing the curtain, opening it again, looking out. He has the urge to call her name, but stops himself. Retreating to the shadows, he sinks hands in his pockets and tries to think.

He owes this woman nothing—he barely knows her—yet some

irksome sliver of memory won't let him walk away. Nothing she said, but a look she gave him. A look that told him everything: that her bed was empty, that she wondered about him, and that anything might happen if he could only be alone with her.

Unable to resist, he glances again at the balcony and finds her there, head upturned, black hair windswept in all directions. Crossing paths with a stray mutt, he traverses the cobblestones at a trot and enters the vestibule of her apartment. He climbs the stairs two at a time. He knocks at her door.

She doesn't answer at once.

"Amnon Halevi here," he calls through a chink in the weathered mahogany. "I was in the neighborhood…"

An obvious subterfuge—what sane Israeli roams about the Muslim Quarter after dark?

Changing tack, he says, "I would have called, but I ran out of *asimonim*. The pay phones on this side of town never seem to work anyway."

She opens the door, not more than a few inches, and stands to one side peering at him with undisguised curiosity.

"You?"

He folds his hands at waist level, shrugs slightly, and waits to be invited in. Drawing her purple velvet robe about her, reknotting the sash, she backs away from the threshold and motions him inside. He enters on tiptoe, his gaze furtively rummaging in every corner of the modest flat.

"Nice place," he says, hoping to cover his indiscretion with a compliment.

"If you're trying to be polite, you needn't bother. Most Israelis don't appreciate these old places. They'd rather live in high-rises. Better satellite reception."

She waves him toward a chair at the kitchen table, its paint chipped and legs rickety. There's an intricately embroidered cloth covering the tabletop and a vase of fresh crocuses at its center.

"Not all Israelis are immune to charm." He feels self-conscious, wishes she'd smile at him the way she once had.

"Aren't you going to ask me what I'm doing living in the Muslim Quarter?"

The question catches him off-guard.

"It does seem odd," he admits.

Turning her back to him, she walks toward an old kerosene stove and lights it.

"I have no coffee—is tea all right?"

"Anything."

She takes a seat beside him. "You're odd yourself, Amnon. Coming here like this. No one but Palestinians brave this neighborhood, especially not at night."

She looks pleased, he decides, though she doesn't smile and doesn't say so. He takes the cup of tea she offers him, grateful for something with which to occupy his hands.

"Aren't you afraid?"

"Afraid?" she responds, as if the word were foreign to her vocabulary. "No one bothers me. I have no enemies."

"No enemies? No enemies?" He strains to keep his voice down. "You're surrounded by enemies. You don't know these people."

"Perhaps it's *you* who don't know them." She crosses the room and draws shut the only window. "Tear gas," she explains, daubing the corner of an eye. A low-flying fighter plane passes overhead with an explosive peal. She doesn't flinch, only lingers at the window with her head upturned, watching it pass. Her voice drifts back to him, "Most people spend their whole lives waging war—against people they don't even know. And against themselves, whom they know least of all."

"You worry me."

He feels her hand rest for a moment on his shoulder.

"My grandfather used to tell me that I had the self-preservation instincts of a moth," she says, smiling at last.

"Well put."

His teacup emptied, he rests his hands on his knees and tries to think of something to say, but the words won't come. She looks so womanly, so vulnerable, sitting there in her nightclothes inches from his grasp. Not trusting himself, he stands and zips up his jacket. "May I come back another time?"

"Yes," she says, her nearness an invitation to linger. "Yes, you must."

"I've had a chat with the American consul about this Cavell woman," announces Shahar.

Amnon's boss, a veteran of five wars captured behind enemy lines and shorn of an eye and both pinkies, swaggers across the office in a single stride and slaps Eve's file onto the desk.

"Turns out she's no kid-glove case, no subversive, no CIA plant, just another confused little Jewish girl with a thing for Arabs." Perching on the desk edge with a proprietary air and failing to notice the grimace that crosses his subordinate's face, he cracks his remaining knuckles and sums up, "Thing to do is call her in and ask a few questions. Put a little scare into her."

Amnon strains backward in his chair, wanting to distance himself from Shahar's one-eyed assault, but the office is too small, the stakes too high.

"Ben Ami's had her under surveillance for five days now," he ventures. "Waste of time. She barely leaves her apartment."

"That doesn't change the fact that she's fallen in with the wrong friends. Sana Mahmoud, for one. I don't need to tell you the headache that bitch has been. That orphanage of hers is nothing but a front. Everyone knows she's got a direct line to Tunis." Shahar pauses to swat at a fly. "Don't underestimate these people, Halevi. The Cavell affair's no shoddy piece of work: wealthy Left-leaning Jew comes to Jerusalem, falls in love with an Arab stud—no doubt a setup, the guy just happens to be Mahmoud's own nephew—and pretty soon she's hanging around this shady orphanage, making generous contributions to the PLO."

"They drew her into a web."

"Exactly," his boss concurs, thumping his fist against the desktop. "Clever of them, one must admit. Not the least bit original, but *clever*."

Amnon scribbles a few notes onto a yellow pad, waiting for Shahar to complete his performance. He's thinking about Eve, picturing her purple robe gliding down the white shoulders. He had been right about her—and wrong. He hadn't expected her to give herself so completely, to give what he'd never learned to ask for and make him wish there were no morning.

Rationing patience, he writes, *Check out nephew*, and utters a feeble, "Cavell looks harmless, if you ask me."

Shahar backs him into a corner with a stabbing motion of his finger stubs.

"I don't care if she's Mother Theresa. We can't afford any more of her monkey business. Call her in, Halevi."

The light dims in Amnon's office. From his desk he hears the usual flurry of hurried goodnights, the sound of file drawers slamming shut and car engines starting. Five p.m. Hour of deliverance.

"Working late, Tiger?"

Gila leans in his doorway, a black sweater draped artlessly across her shoulder, one spike-heeled shoe kicked off.

Amnon points with his chin toward the in-box, still half full.

"It's just paper, Halevi."

"No," he counters glumly, "it's people's lives."

The secretary cowers in mock terror.

"Don't tell me you're developing a messiah complex, like the mighty Shahar." Kicking off the other shoe, she pads into the office and drops into the one straight-backed chair. "What are you doing here, anyway, Halevi? This is no place for a rich boy with brains."

Amnon shrugs.

"The situation isn't good."

"So, what else is new?" Swinging one stockinged foot onto his desk, she tips the chair back at what seems to Amnon a precarious angle, and runs a hand through her coiffed platinum blonde hair. "Me, I got a daughter to support. I'm not looking to save the world."

Amnon strains to keep his eyes from her knees, which are raised and parted beyond the limits of propriety. With Eve's folder still in his hands, he stands and begins to pace.

"You talk as if I'm some naive adolescent," he says, dissembling his annoyance only partially.

"You don't belong here, Halevi, that's all I'm saying. Just look around. There are two major food groups in this outfit—your basic brute in blinders and the Zen type, detached and soft in the belly." She lowers the chair, rises, and steps into her shoes. "You're neither."

Seized by a terrible clarity, he places the folder in the out-basket and reaches for his leather jacket.

"I owe you a cup of coffee."

She winks at him once from the doorway and saunters off, trailing her maddening perfume.

#

Amnon turns the corner onto Saffron Street and, tensing at the sound of his own footfalls, searches the shadows for Ben Ami. The acne-faced agent, conspicuous as gunmetal in his gray trench coat, stands against a stone wall with a crumpled copy of *Al Quds* tucked under an arm for effect.

Amnon greets him with a fleeting arch of the eyebrows.

"Any action?"

"Does a legless man jump puddles?" the agent rejoins with a grunt. "*Shumdeval*, nothing. She hasn't come down." He motions Amnon closer and snickers, "Crazy broad puts on music and dances around in front of the windows. I've seen her tits a couple of times."

Amnon feels his gut clench.

"Look," he says with forced camaraderie, "you must be bored stiff. Why don't I relieve you for an hour? Go to Jaffa Road, have a cup of coffee. It will help keep you awake."

Ben Ami claps Amnon on the back.

"You won't tell Shahar?"

"This is between us," Amnon assures him.

He watches his colleague walk briskly along the cobbled street and vanish into the souk. He gazes up at Eve's balcony, half expecting to find her there, but the windows are dark, the curtains drawn tight. A feral cat drops from the roof onto a window ledge and scratches at the pane. A light flickers on. Eve's silhouette flashes against the diaphanous curtain, moving to a rhythm inaudible from the pavement below.

Racing across the street, he enters the shadowy vestibule and bounds up the staircase. As he reaches the landing her door opens and he hears her murmur, "I didn't think you'd come back."

"You don't know your own power."

He allows her to lead him inside. A blues collection moans on the CD player, ballads as dark as the moonless night. She dances away from him with a beckoning look, lips parted, not quite smiling.

"Why *did* you come back?"

He shrinks into a corner, leans one shoulder against the wall. "People don't always need reasons."

The glimmer of a smile crosses her lips.

"You're a hard man to know, Amnon. Stony, like this city. But even you can't hide forever; sooner or later someone's bound to chip away your defenses."

She drops her purple robe, then the filmy silk chemise beneath it. Naked, she leads him across the threshold of her bedroom and lights a candle.

Giddy with desire, paralyzed by conscience, he stops short.

"We have to talk," he says miserably.

She nestles against him, her bare skin breaking down his resolve. Like a man colliding with himself, he tears the sheet from the bed and wraps her in it with as much tenderness as his rough hands can muster. "There's something you need to know."

Braced against the bedpost with his chin sunk on his chest, he gropes for words.

"The way you've been living here—the very fact that you've chosen to live here—isn't normal. It doesn't sit right with…certain people."

"I don't care what people think."

"I'm not talking about just anyone, I'm talking about the authorities. Look, Israel isn't New Zealand. You can't come here and hang out with the Arabs and whatever else, and not arouse suspicion."

She tosses back her hair.

"You sound like a cop."

"I *am* a cop." He veers to face her.

They freeze in this position, she glaring at him through narrowed eyes, he feeling the distance between them crack open like a seismic rift.

"I have your file," he says finally.

"What are you, Amnon, some kind of male Mata Hari? Is that why you came here? To fuck a confession out of me?"

He reaches out a hand and tries to stroke her cheek, but she backs away from him.

"I wanted to help you—I still want to help you. Your Arab friends have tricked you, they've taken advantage of your generosity. You're a pawn in a very dangerous game."

"Are you talking about Sana?"

He nods.

"Sana is as straight as they come," she says, her voice sharp with defiance. "She runs an orphanage. Is there any law against that?"

"There's more going on at that orphanage than you know."

Eve bolts to her feet and strides to the door with the bed sheet trailing behind.

"I don't have to talk to you."

"No, you don't have to. In fact, you could report me and have me fired. I have no business being here."

He follows, crazy to touch her, to begin all over again. Her skin whispers to him. It smells of spice, of places he's never been. With back turned to him she retrieves the chemise from the rug and pulls it on.

"You never let down your guard, do you?" She re-drapes the sheet across her shoulders with a modesty that tells him he's lost ground. "Even when you're making love."

"If something matters enough, you defend it. That's the way it is here."

She goes on, as if she's not heard him.

"I was so happy the night you showed up at my door. I'd thought about you so many times—those soulful eyes, the quiet way you spoke…"

"I only want to help you."

He watches the set of her shoulders slacken, hears her sigh into the folds of gathered muslin. For a moment he dares to hope that she might turn to him, cry or laugh or lift her lips to be kissed.

"All you'd have to do is say you didn't know what you were getting into," he pleads with her, "that you had no idea who Sana was. I'd get you off. You could stay in Jerusalem, move to a quiet neighborhood like Rehavia or Yemin Moshe."

"I know perfectly well who Sana is and I know what she wants—the same things you or I want. Dignity. A home. A future for the orphans."

"Pretty words, but we're talking security."

Hardened into someone he no longer knows, she faces him with arms folded across her bosom and lips drawn taut.

"So tell me, Officer Halevi, what have I done to deserve all this attention? What nasty evidence have you got in that file?"

"According to our intelligence, you've been seen on numerous occasions with Mahmoud. You spend time at her orphanage. From all appearances, you've been giving money to the PLO."

He waits for her to respond, but instead she takes his jacket from a chair back and holds it out to him.

"Good-bye, Amnon."

"That's it?"

"What were you expecting? A signed and sworn affidavit?"

He takes the jacket and tosses it back onto the chair. He holds out his arms to her. "We can get through this. I'll stand by you."

Eve makes no move, only draws her arms more tightly about her.

"There's an orphan Sana's taken in," she says in a voice stung with sorrow, "a little girl named Samira. She shakes all over, hides at the smallest sound. I've become her godmother. I want to see her get well. I've provided for her education. Now you know."

She walks to the front door and opens it.

"Good-bye, Amnon," she says again, lowering her eyes as he trudges past her into the beam of a single bare bulb.

Gila places the freshly typed letter in an envelope and hands it to Amnon, saying, "You sure about this?"

He nods. Having passed the night sleepless, his eyelids feel heavy and his head light. Seizing the offensive, he takes the letter and heads directly for Shahar's office.

He finds his boss hunched over a towering stack of files, a look of fierce concentration on his tired face.

"Problem, Halevi?" he says without glancing up.

"No problem." Amnon slides the letter across his desk.

"As if I don't have enough to read—what's this about?"

"My letter of resignation, sir."

Shahar heaves the files to a side and motions Amnon into a seat.

"What's going on with you, anyway? Family problems? Money problems? A broken heart? I've been meaning to have a schmooze with you."

Amnon seats himself at the edge of a metal folding chair. Shahar, reaching into his breast pocket for a Marlboro, lurches to his feet and closes the office door.

"Just between us," the veteran says in a voice raspy from too much smoking, "there are days I don't feel like coming here myself. A glamour job this isn't, but somebody's got to do it. The Arabs think they can wear us down—that's been their strategy all along—but we Israelis are like the cactus fruit. Tough when we need to be."

Amnon, not wanting to prolong the conversation, says simply,

"I'm not right for this job."

"Not right? With your army record?" As Shahar speaks, his four-fingered hands tear open the envelope. "You fit the profile perfectly. I hired you myself. Something's eating you, that's all; hemorrhoids maybe, or—don't tell me—a girlfriend from the peace camp. I've heard it all, my boy. You can't shock me."

Shahar's vulpine eye scans the letter, blinking as it reaches bottom.

Amnon removes his holster and places it on the desk edge. He wonders what it would be like to turn a blind corner without feeling his back prickle or to make love in a field of wildflowers.

"An elegant smokescreen, Halevi," the old vet says with mock admiration, "this *ideological dilemma* of yours. Care to talk about it?"

"No, sir," Amnon responds evenly.

Unable to suppress a smile he gets to his feet and walks out of Shahar's office, down the airless corridors and past the closed-circuit cameras, into a world of possibility.

POSTHUMOUS MEETINGS

I tzik Koenig catches his first glimpse of Jerusalem from the back seat of a crowded *sherut* and thinks, what a ghastly place to die. The timeworn facades and sudden stretches of nothingness recall Pest after the War, the sting of going home to a rubble-strewn flat stripped of its last curtain hook and watching his father open and close the windows a thousand times, as if suffocating or scavenging the fetid air. He and his twin brother, David, had shuffled from room to room in bewilderment, listening to him inventory aloud the missing contents: a chiffonier that had held their baby clothes, *Baba* Sadie's silver candelabra, the piano that had been their mother's pride...As the list grew too long to contemplate, the loss too immense to bear, they clapped hands to their ears. They yelled, "You're not our papa!" and demanded to be taken back to the peasants' cottage where they had spent the Holocaust years living as gentile children in bland ignorance of their lousy fortune.

The memory only exacerbates Itzik's first impression of Jerusalem and makes him wish he hadn't come. That his father had chosen to spend his last years in this ruin of a city, he can only marvel. As the unwieldy taxi lurches from pothole to pothole and the morning glare bleaches the landscape a forlorn shade of nowhere, he draws in his elbows and resolves—at the very first pay phone—to book a flight back to Hungary.

Itzik rouses reluctantly from a nap. His groggy eyes scan the dim hotel room, searching for the telling detail that will reveal his location. Fumbling for the room service menu, he focuses on the cryptic

Hebrew script, an alphabet he has only seen in prayer books. Being of rational mind, he has never understood his *landsleit*'s insistence on resurrecting a dead language with no application to technology and no curse words.

"*Butasag*, these crazy people," he mutters under his breath. "Why don't they chisel *steak, omelettes, Coca-Cola* onto a stone tablet and drag it up Mount Sinai, for chrissake?"

Wriggling into a silk bathrobe patterned after a leopard's hide, he lumbers to his feet and pads across the shag carpet to a window. Rush-hour traffic inches along King George Street.

Pedestrians race down the sidewalks with newspapers and shopping sacks under their arms. He glances at his Doxa, which is still on Hungarian time, and surmises that the day has ended and the evening begun. The sun hovers just above the parapets of the YMCA, gilding the street with its waning glow. His father would have set a scene in such light. The moment just before darkness.

Mozes Koenig—Partisan, professor, anguished storyteller—was never more than a silhouette to his sons. When Itzik thinks about him now, he pictures a bearish man seated in an armchair reading aloud by candlelight, his voice so vacant that it might belong to a zombie.

He spoke only once of their mother, Gizella, shot dead en route to Dachau for singing a lullaby to a frightened child. He waited until they turned thirteen, the supposed juncture at which a boy becomes a man, and on the pretense of commemorating the occasion took them to the neighborhood pastry shop. His craving for sweets had considerably inflated his girth by then. He had begun to wax and purl the tips of his mustache.

"You're old enough to know the truth," he told them, stalling, tugging nervously at his facial hair, while they devoured a last plateful of dobostorta and apricot strudel. "You're old enough to know…what people are capable of."

To Itzik's embarrassment, he had broken down sobbing, this bear of a man who some considered a hero. People stared. David scraped the whipped cream from his father's untouched raspberry tart and threw his soiled napkin onto the table. "The War's over. What difference does it make now?"

His father stopped reading aloud to them after that—he all but stopped speaking to them. Once he'd supervised their homework and their hygiene, he would retire to his bedroom and close the door behind him. Itzik could hear him wind an alarm clock, fluff the pillows, and then silence. The same silence that surrounds him here. The same shut-out feeling.

Tomorrow he will bury his father, he muses bitterly, the father who in life has already been dead to him for four decades.

He takes an electronic notebook from his briefcase and enters *Halevi, Leah*. An Israeli friend of his father's, someone Itzik has never met but to whom he's indebted for the funeral arrangements. He takes the telephone onto his lap and marks her phone number.

"*Halo?*" responds a woman's voice edged by static.

Itzik responds in correct, if self-conscious, English, "This is Itzik Koenig. I am in Jerusalem and—"

"Good, join us for dinner. You have the address."

He showers hurriedly, cuts himself shaving, and styles his thinning hair with gel. The mirror casts back the image of a middle-aged man who wears his years with no particular grace, neither fat nor thin, defined solely by brooding brown eyes and downturned lips. Not bad for half a century, he consoles himself, pressing moistened toilet tissue onto the nicks.

The telephone buzzes, brokenly, as if transmitting in Morse Code. Racing naked and expectant into the next room, he picks up the receiver and listens as a synthesized voice drones, "This is your wake-up call, your wake-up call, your wake-up call..."

A vigorous woman with fiery auburn hair and dimpled cheeks ushers Itzik to a cluttered table.

"No need to stand on ceremony," she chides as he bends forward to kiss her hand.

He draws himself up with wounded pride. "Silly anachronism. Must have picked it up from my father."

"Ah, your father. I've never known anyone like him." She motions Itzik toward a chair. "Hope you don't mind leftovers. My husband, Jacob, is working late at the office and I wasn't expecting company."

"Frankly," he admits, "I don't have much of an appetite tonight."

Her features soften, and Itzik notes the benign set of her rounded shoulders.

"Of course. This must be difficult for you, coming all this way. When had you last seen Mozes?"

Itzik feels his face redden.

"Five, six...maybe seven years ago."

Neither he nor his twin brother had visited their father once he settled in Jerusalem. David had been too busy making money, and Itzik too busy managing it for him. An occasional phone call had been sufficient to assuage the conscience. Mozes wouldn't have expected more.

"But, to lose him so suddenly," Leah says in a surfeit of compassion. A single tear rolls languidly down her cheek. "Such a senseless death. Mozes would have hated the inanity of it."

"The casket will be closed, I assume?"

"I didn't see him. Jacob went to the morgue to identify the—the remains." She pushes a covered casserole dish toward him. "But you must eat *something*."

"The knife wounds," Itzik can't keep himself from asking, "how many were there? Five? Ten? More?"

Leah lowers her fork.

"I don't know. I didn't read the coroner's report and the papers didn't say. Apparently, the Arab came at them in some kind of frenzy. Innocent people—most of them old, like your father—just waiting for a bus."

"Stunned, they had to have been."

"In broad daylight. Jaffa Road is jammed with people and cars at that hour. Who would have imagined…?"

Itzik pushes his chair back from the table and takes a dented box of Pall Malls from his trouser pocket. Staring at a blank spot on the wall, he lights up.

"That's better," he sighs.

Leah uncorks a wine bottle.

"Tokaji?"

"I don't imbibe," he says. Then, with a wink, "But perhaps I'll start. Life is so full of upsets."

"You have your father's sense of humor."

Itzik hunches forward onto his elbows, as if the remark had thumped him on the back.

"I wouldn't know."

Leah looks at him, her eyes overcast like the winter sky. Itzik has the urge to bare his heart to her and confess everything, the years of estrangement, the things left unsaid, the son he'd not been.

"I never really knew my father," he says in a clipped voice, and can say no more.

Mozes' publisher has asked Itzik to write a foreword to the two novels that comprise the whole of his father's literary legacy. The manuscripts are in his briefcase. He has yet to read them.

"It's really too ironic. For years no one in Hungary paid the least attention to my father's work. Even other survivors—his own friends—thought him extreme, off the mark. You couldn't give his book away. Now that he's been stabbed to death by some Islamic zealot, overnight he's become all the rage, virtually a cult figure."

Leah winces.

"Here, he was loved. His first book, A Time for War—" she motions absently toward a bookcase "—spoke to the heart of every Israeli mother. The characters were as real to us as our own families. When Hannah lost Shlomo, we mourned with her. And when our own sons were about to become soldiers, we left the book beside their beds, hoping it would say what we couldn't find the words for."

"How odd, then, that the sequel was so long in coming."

"Nearly forty years."

"People dry up."

"Not Mozes," Leah says sharply, inclining toward him with a look of challenge in her eyes. "Your father had a fertile imagination, but he was a survivor, don't forget. He had things to sort out. As time passed he began to question all his earlier conclusions, then to question even his questions. He drifted from his public. These last years he lived almost as a hermit."

Itzik snuffs out his cigarette and collapses against the chair back.

"His latest novel—what do you make of it?"

"Literary suicide."

"I don't understand."

"I'm not sure that I understand either. Your father wasn't an easy man to second-guess." She stands and begins to clear dishes from the table. "Tea or coffee?"

He trails her into the kitchen.

"A Time for Peace...is that not the title of the new book? Sounds like he turned 180 degrees."

"Exactly," Leah concurs.

Ignoring him, she sets a teakettle on the stove and begins to rifle through the cupboards for honey and tinned biscuits.

"Every author has his Muse," he continues to ruminate. "Someone must have inspired my father's comeback. Was there a woman?"

"I'd hardly call her a Muse, but yes, it seems that he met some young American and became obsessed with her—for lack of a better term, she's the novel's heroine. It's a hackneyed story, pathetic really: quasi-Jewish poet comes to Jerusalem to find her roots and ends up shtupping an Arab." She veers to face him. "Look, your father was a great man. So, maybe he lost his marbles toward the end. That's no reason to dismiss his earlier achievements."

Itzik drops into a chair.

"You might as well know," he says with a shrug. "The publisher's doing a print run of 100,000 on the new book, he's sold foreign rights in twenty different countries, and there's talk of a movie."

Leah shrugs in turn.

"Everything about your father's life defies logic."

The desert landscape, streaming past the windshield like an unfinished canvas, echoes the arid sprawl of Itzik's thoughts. From the passenger seat of Leah's late-model Honda, he watches Jerusalem recede into the background and a patchwork of stony fields, most lying fallow, press back the horizon.

Almost cheerful after a night's rest and a hearty Israeli-style breakfast, Itzik reconstructs what he knows of his father's life—that he was born in 1921 under the sign of Leo to a prosperous baker and his artist wife, that he married at the age of seventeen, went off with the Partisans three years later, and came back a shadow of himself.

But *who* was Mozes Koenig? All those years he lived behind a closed door, what dreams and demons might have been battling for his soul?

"Jacob could have pulled some strings to get Mozes into the cemetery on Mount Herzl," Leah says, the throaty resonance of her voice rousing Itzik from his reveries, "but we thought he would have preferred to be somewhere less crowded."

Leaving the car to one side of a rustic gatepost, they alight and begin the short walk to the graveyard.

"A lot of people today are choosing to be buried on the kib-butzim," adds her husband, steering Itzik briskly by an elbow. "It's more economical."

Itzik inhales the clean bracing air.

"I've never understood all the fuss Jews make about the dead. The living have a hard enough time. Why dwell on one's losses?"

Leah, her red-rimmed eyes shooting sparks, tramps ahead.

"Something I said?" Itzik appeals to Jacob.

The Israeli gives him an awkward pat on the shoulder.

"Not to worry. My wife had a soft spot for your father."

They walk in silence to a crudely excavated grave surrounded by wild poppies. Beside it, the simple oak coffin that bears Mozes' defaced corpse gathers flies and dust.

For a moment Itzik has an urge to retrace his steps, to shed the role of bereaved son and find a sunny patch of ground where he might stretch out and take a nap, but his eyes fix on the sorry-looking wooden box and won't be pried away. A brawny man in work clothes strides forward to shake his hand. He murmurs a few words in Hebrew, which Itzik doesn't understand, then retires on squeaky rubber soles to a discreet distance and leans against a tree trunk.

"He's head of the kibbutz council," Jacob explains. "He'll con-duct a brief ceremony—strictly secular, of course. From what we can gather, your father remained an atheist to the end."

As Itzik mulls over this latest revelation, an elderly woman, heavily veiled, approaches with brittle dignity. Nodding to the other mourners, she extracts an elaborate lace fan from her purse and proceeds to ventilate herself with mincing flicks of the wrist.

Itzik looks inquiringly at Jacob.

"I wouldn't have expected to see *her* here," Jacob whispers. "She's the widow of an influential politician. According to rumor, for a short time at least, she was in love with Mozes. Whatever there was between them didn't come to much. She hasn't spoken to him in years."

Itzik's gaze drifts from the widow's fan to the coffin to the poppies. His mind frames questions. Had his father loved this woman, jilted her? Once the War ended, was he capable of loving *anyone*?

A grim-faced man in uniform, one eye obscured by a black eyepatch, limps up to Jacob and claps him on the back. As the man retracts his hands, Itzik notes that he is missing not one but both pinkies.

"Is this the deceased's son?" the old soldier asks in oddly accented English. Without waiting for a response, he takes Itzik by the sleeve. "Colonel Koenig was a credit to this nation." He holds out a blue and white pouch imprinted with the initials IDF. "On behalf of the Israeli Defense Forces," he says, as if reading an edict, "I present you with this flag, so that your father can be buried as a hero deserves to be."

Itzik thanks him with an abbreviated bow and turns with raised eyebrows to Jacob.

"Israel doesn't forget its Partisans." He relieves Itzik of the parcel. "Your father's sudden dovishness didn't exactly endear him to the army, but all that's forgotten now. Some of his old cronies on the Right are trying to use his death to push for a harder line against the Arabs. Not much Mozes can do about it now." Regarding the pouch with what seems to Itzik exaggerated reverence, he sadly shakes his head. "I'll see about draping the coffin."

Jacob walks off, leaving Itzik to stand sheepishly beside Leah. For what seem eons they stare at the hole in the ground, avoiding each other's eyes.

Itzik has an incipient case of indigestion. He feels a heaviness at his center, the cloying weight of questions left unasked and unanswered. Once all the stories have been told and the few slim truths tallied, who was Mozes Koenig—lover or fighter?

"That mustache of his," he says absently, "it hinted at a certain devil-may-care, something inside that never quite found expression in his life."

"He was his own most colorful character." Leah's voice softens. "You had to know him. You had to hear him tell a story or watch him eat a meal. Everything tickled him; he left nothing unsavored, not a crumb."

"I never saw that side of him."

"Not many people did."

"Did my father ever speak of us," he wonders aloud, "of my brother and me?"

"Made you sound like a couple of big shot capitalists, always on the run."

"Did he sound—did he seem—proud of us?"

"Yes, certainly," she hastens to assure him but then looks embarrassed, has nothing more to say.

For another interminable stretch they stand side by side in a doleful silence, Leah daubing at her eyes with a tissue, Itzik feeling his stomach anchor him to the present like a penance. Without warning Leah nudges him on the arm and points with her chin toward the approaching figure of a young dark-haired woman wrapped from neck to hips in a black shawl.

"It's *her*. Your father's Muse."

The first thing Itzik notices about Eve is her hands. He finds the
pale vulnerability of them so affecting, so tragic, that he can't look
away.

"You're staring," Leah chides him in a whisper.

Itzik lowers his gaze to the coffin.

"She reminds me of someone."

Leah, her voice tinged by rancor, replies, "Careful, Itzik. That's
what your father said."

The brief ceremony concluded, Itzik excuses himself on the pretext of needing to spend time alone at his father's grave. As the rest
of the mourners disperse, walking hurriedly toward parked cars, he
trudges in widening laps about the half-buried coffin, his sights fixed
on Eve. She has left the cemetery and meandered into a field of
swaying grasses. At a distance she pauses and removes the black
shawl, revealing shoulders even more pale and delicate than her
hands. Itzik watches, blind to everything but these shoulders. He circles the grave and begins to cross the field, heedlessly trampling
flowers, not seeing and not caring.

At his approach Eve veers toward him with a startled expression.
She's been crying, he quickly surmises, and just as quickly begins to
imagine what it would be like to draw her into his arms and taste her
tears.

"Please," he says, proffering his monogrammed linen handkerchief.

She takes it only after he insists, and turns to him with a smile
so poignant it might be made of fallen stars.

"I just can't believe he's gone."

Her gaze rests on his face, penetrating the mask of mourning he's
hidden behind since his arrival. She surprises him by saying, "You

must be one of Mozes' sons."

"None other." For once he is glad of his parentage and the bearish looks that mark him as his father's heir. "Itzik Koenig," he introduces himself, hastily plucking a poppy and handing it to her with his signature bow. "And you?" He feigns ignorance. "How did you know my father?"

"Shall we walk?" she rejoins, continuing her earlier trajectory.

Preening his lapels, he falls into step alongside her.

"I didn't know your father very long," she says in a tone of confession. "We met one morning this past winter, walking through the souk. We took to each other, as strangers sometimes do in such settings, and spent the afternoon pouring out our life stories."

"Oh?"

"Actually, Mozes did most of the talking. Your father's life had the pathos of epic poetry. What hadn't he seen? The stories he told..."

"Of course. Others have said that very thing."

"He seemed lonely. He did a lot of roaming. I'd see him pass by my balcony, sometimes two or three times in a single day. He'd leave bouquets on the sidewalk, hum rhapsodies, and then move on. Dogs would follow him, children...he had a kind word for everyone and everything."

Itzik stops walking.

"A kind word—how many times as a boy I needed one. Where were his kind words then? What sort of father closes the door on his own son?"

"He spoke about you and your twin brother—David, isn't that his name? You two meant the world to him. He told me about leaving you with the gentile family and how he counted the days until he could go back and fetch you. You were all he had left after the War. You kept the happy memories of his life with your mother alive for him. You kept *him* alive."

"Alive? Have you ever seen a living ghost? That was my father after the War, and for many years after that."

The poppy falls from Eve's hand, its petals escaping on the breeze.

"Look, I may not have known your father for very long, but he confided in me. I know things others who were closer to him might not."

"Tell me," Itzik begs in a small voice, the voice of the lonely child he had once been.

"I don't need to tell you that it took all the strength your father could muster just to fend off the temptation of suicide those first years back in Pest. He was never able to love again after your mother. His profession didn't fulfill him. But despite all the empty years, all he had lost, he died believing in some divine force, in something more powerful than hatred and violence. That's why he wrote *A Time for Peace*."

"Yes, yes…surely that's how it was."

"I'm sorry, Itzik. I'm sorry it had to end this way."

He looks up, beyond the rooftops, beyond the tenuous realm of will, and feeling himself hollow and forsaken shakes his fists in the air.

"My father died believing—but what of us who survive him? How are we to believe in a God who lets old people be hacked to death at a bus stop?"

"Mozes might have had an answer," she ventures. "But then again, maybe not. What was it that finally earned your father his immortality, after all? Not his books. His polemics?—people had heard it all before. No, Mozes Koenig will be remembered for the questions he posed. In death as in life."

"Questions—is that to be my inheritance?"

She gives him a look that disarms even as it stings.

"You disregard example."

"I know what you're thinking: that I'm an ingrate, a bad son, *no son*. Perhaps you're right."

"Forgive him, Itzik. Forgive yourself."

He captures her hand, turns it over in his own. They begin once more to walk. A distant laughter mingles with the whistle of wind through grass, with Eve's cadenced footfalls. He looks up to see a group of overall-clad kibbutzniks cross the cemetery in loose formation, voices raised in debate and a burlap bag of oranges passing from hand to hand.

"What a strange place, this *homeland*," he says, shaking his head. "I've never felt myself so foreign."

Eve smiles. "I know the feeling. Your father and I used to talk about it. Had he lived, he might very well have gone back to Hungary."

"And you?"

"My bags are packed."

"Where will you go? Back to America?"

"Eventually."

"But surely," he insists, "you have a destination."

"Meteora...the Uluguru Mountains...Dakar...Punta Piedras..." She speaks the names with a strange tenderness. Her eyes strain against the horizon as if to jar it loose.

He would follow her, if he could.

"Changchun...Mandalay...Land's End..."

The poppies ripple and tease. Migrating raptors tear pieces from the sky. Mozes would have set a love scene in just such a field at just such a moment, but Itzik's timing is off. Already he feels Eve drifting from him, part of her gone even as their shadows merge, part of her so distant she might never have been there at all.

"Before you go, there's one thing you must tell me. You reminded my father of someone. Who was it?"

"Why, your mother, of course," she replies, turning from him with a flourish of her shawl. "I reminded him of Gizella."

Itzik Koenig boards a *sherut* bound for Ben-Gurion airport. As the crowded taxi winds its way into the Judean hills, he snaps open his attaché case and extracts a manuscript. His eyes scan the title page.

"What are you reading?" asks a little Hassidic boy huddled in the seat beside him.

"A book."

"I know it's a book," the boy rejoins, tossing his forelocks with impatience. "What's it about?"

"I'm not sure," says Itzik, "but one day I'll figure it out."

Returning his attention to the manuscript, he hears his father read aloud in his ghostlike voice, *For my beloved sons, who inherited my big feet but were spared the journey,* and watches in wonder as the words seep down the page, their edges softened by his own tears.

ACKNOWLEDGMENTS

I went to Jerusalem a journalist and came back a novelist. Sometime between the stabbings of old people on Jaffa Road and the demise of the militant rabbi, Meir Kahane, I cut my press card to shreds with a pair of cuticle scissors. My carefully measured column inches, aptly called "hard news," had failed miserably to capture the region's complex moral climate, the questions posed in equal parts by its beauty and its brutality.

If, in *Between Two Deserts*, I have managed to add dimension and nuance to the media images, credit must go first and foremost to the people of Israel and Palestine, especially to those who, without having known a single day of peace, model it so well. Their resilience and willingness to continue seeking solutions humble me.

Special thanks to the New Israel Fund for its aid in connecting me to the region's extensive network of grassroots peace and coexistence groups, and to the Society for the Preservation of Nature in Israel for sponsoring my trek across the Negev Desert and enabling me to meet the very embodiment of peace, the Dalai Lama.

I am indebted to the Arizona Commission on the Arts, who, in 1998, awarded an early version of *Between Two Deserts* my state's literary fellowship in fiction, and to the book's first shepherds, Laurence Jordan and Sydelle Kramer.

Kudos to my socio-linguistic advisors, Cesare Frustaci, Adel Soliman Gamal, David Liss, and cyber-angel Viktor for the myriad details of time and tongue, and to fellow writers Martha Moutray, Vera Marie Badertscher, Shay Salomon, and Amy Weintraub for extending my worldview. To David Poindexter and the preternaturally literate staff at MacAdam/Cage, a standing ovation for preserving what is most precious in publishing—the love of a good read.

Back home in my own desert, I look out at the current situation in the Middle East with a sorrow mitigated by faith in the essential goodness of people and their potential for transcendence. I am grateful to live surrounded by friends. Together we weave a vision of the possible, and the blue of the desert sky soothes away all qualm.